PREFACE

The children and their puppies of CLOCKWORK STRANGE

Daniel	09 yrs. old
Jacob	09 yrs. old
Beverly	09 yrs. old
Benny	08 yrs. old
Devin	08 yrs. old
Georgi	08 yrs. old
Gordon	06 yrs. old
Vera	06 yrs. old
Di-Di	05 yrs. old

Mickey	Black Cocker Spaniel
Skipper	Black and White Cocker Spaniel
Towzer	Border Collie

BIOPIC of CLOCKWORK STRANGE

Dale is an artist from Southern Alberta that mostly deals in palaeo art. His early recollections of life were growing up on a farm outside the little hamlet of La Riviere [Larvyer] in Manitoba, Canada. For this reason he became a Nature lover. In his novel CLOCKWORK STRANGE, he recounts what life was like from the 1930s to 50s living on one of these prairie farms through the eyes of 9 children and their 3 puppies.

As a child Dale was fascinated by dinosaurs and deep time. The release of Karel Zeman's 1955 "Cesta Do Praveku" movie of 4 children lost in time on their grandparents' farm where they find a door to ancient worlds, long since dead, struck a particularly personal chord with this author. Combined with his life long fascination in the palaeontology of deep time and his 10 years of professional work with some of Canada's finest museums, both in the lab and in the field ... the author wishes to take the reader back through 4.55 billion years of our planet's history. Each novel will represent a distinct geological Stage of time in our planet's history lasting 5 to 6 million years. Each one will be experienced through the eyes of 9 children during their stay in each stage of Earth's history.

What is unique about the telling of the tale CLOCKWORK STRANGE is that it is based on actual towns and farm communities of the 1930s - 50s. Virtually all the characters themselves inhabiting the novel CLOCKWORK STRANGE are real characters taken from real life [names have been altered]. Many are long since deceased.

As of the writing of the first novel, of the 9 children in it, only 8 are alive today. The puppies Mickey, Skipper and Towzer, their real names, were once real dogs. They were all deceased as far back as the 1950s. This is a story of a North American farm community of the 1930s – 50s.

This spellbinding novel is total fiction placed upon a real template of people and towns as the author once remembered them. To some extent, the novel is an epithet to those people. It is also set up as a series to educate young children of all ages on the concept of deep time. It is done as if Karel Zeman himself had written it, had he been alive today, in the 21st C, but armed with our present day knowledge of deep time.

DEDICATION

I dedicate CLOCKWORK STRANGE to the late Karel Zeman whose 1955 children's film Cesta do Praveku so inspired me to search for a career in palaeontology.

This dedication is also extended to the Canadian subsidiary of the American Kellogg Company who introduced me to dinosaurs in 1953 through their give away toy packages in every box of Rice Krispies. To this day, I can no longer eat Rice Krispies, as I probably consumed 10% of their annual production quota.

I also wish a special dedication to the creators and artists who kept another dinosaur series going that inspired many children in the 1950s to enter palaeontology, the motion pictures and further enhanced their enthusiasms towards writing, drawing and painting.

Yes. I am calling out to the creators, who lifted my imagination to soaring heights while I lived on the farm scouring my favourite children's comic book icon ... Turok, son of stone [later ... warrior].

To my favourite person ... my mom ... Edythe Catherine McInnes ... who made all this possible.

Forever in your debt.

THE SIGHTING

Albert opened his eyes. He was lying face down among the five foot reeds of the slough. He was conscious again and gasped as a man deprived for sometime of air. He brought his head up and with all the willpower that he could muster, slowly staggered to his feet. He gasped heavily as he peered out at the landscape, beyond the reeds. He tried to steady himself as he slowly turned around for a full three hundred sixty degrees attempting to get his bearings. He stopped suddenly; he was in shock, unable to comprehend what he saw. It couldn't possibly be ... it couldn't. The farmhouse, roads, telegraph poles, and that terrifying derelict of a caboose ... the instigator of it all ... it was still all there.

Everything he remembered from his past was staring back at him from the yawning chasm of time ... of ancient memories. It couldn't be. It was as if providence had suddenly released its grip on him. He held his breath trying to take it all in, he was back. It still looked as he remembered it in 1943. Perhaps nothing had changed. He was hoping so. It had been for Albert, a harrowing twenty long tumultuous intervening years since his disappearance and simultaneous re-appearance in 1943.

Yet, here he was.

Time had not passed for those here in 1943 unlike what Albert had just endured. He was still wearing the bow across his chest with a quiver of arrows strapped to his back. His clothes were hanging off his frame in tattered strips; his scalp and facial hair were as one. He was unrecognizable. Albert was overcome with delirious excitement. His emotions swelled quickly to the surface of his psyche.

"My god, my god ... I'm here ... I'm here ... I'm really here ..."

Albert's eyes began to water and the moisture started to careen down his cheeks. He was fighting for emotional control when he caught sight of his young nephew, ten year old Eduard, half a mile away, pedaling on his bike like a demon possessed, up the old dirt road leading to the old farmyard. He yelled out to Eduard several times ... to no avail. Albert's heart was pounding, he was utterly exhausted.

Albert lowered his head to his chest as his knees collapsed back onto the ground bringing him down once again, deep within the reeds. Albert trembled as he wept and looked back up at the blue sky overhead and whispered...

"I'm home ... I'm finally home ..."

It is summer ... 1943...

For miles around ... there were vast wheat fields surrounding the little town of La Riviere. They were dotted with many small farms, operated by the Morley clan. Two such farms, up on the prairie escarpment overlooking La Riviere, were themselves located on opposite sides of a large slough or marshland big enough to be called a small lake.

Residents around La Riviere knew it as Morley Lake. Our saga begins on the farm owned by Albert's brother, old timer William [Willie] James Morley and his wife Mable.

Willie J. was a tall, imposing man, square jawed, ruggedly handsome with a low, soft voice. He was a stereotypical farmer who knew the land, was an all round handyman and builder, cigar chomping, pipe smoking, tobacco chewing and religious type, but not overly so. He was a jovial spirit and mostly kept to himself. Mable was his counter match...a small woman, stern, a baker for church bazaars, gardener along with her husband, very religious, organizer of social functions and centre of the family.

Willie J. and his wife Mable had acquired this small section of land adjacent to what was to become the future Lake Morley ... a tear drop shaped slough some three thousand feet across where cattle and horses could come down and drink. It was also somewhat of a wildlife sanctuary where geese and mallards and the occasional swan would take refuge...perhaps even nest. Willie and Mable were in their 40s. They had inherited a rather narrow, but tall two story house with a couple of gardens and a hedge surrounding it all.

The hedge was designed to keep out the long, icy cold, ever windy winter winds that blew incessantly on such unprotected desolate places across the prairies of Canada. The large pine evergreens framed the courtyard surrounding the little white wooden house. Over time, Willie J. with his sons, built some five barns, two chicken coops, a couple of small tool sheds and a pump house for spring water.

In the evenings, Willie J. would sit on his favourite sofa by the kitchen window at night reading the Winnipeg Free Press newspaper. He would take off his glasses and put down his newspaper whenever he heard the forlorn whistle of a steam engine in the middle of the beautiful starry nights somewhere far away on the prairie landscape. It was to him the loneliest sound one could ever hear in a lifetime ... like the howling of long dead souls still wandering those dark nights across the prairies. It was at once beautiful and hauntingly sad.

A very long fence of grey posts and barbed wire wrapped itself around Morley Lake and accompanied by a long dirt road worn into the landscape by tire tracks. It was this dirt road that connected the two farms on one side of the lake. The dirt road continued to wrap itself around the farmyard of Willie J's, extending itself down the other side of Morley Lake to join a municipal gravel road which framed the other side of this water-shed. This gravel road lead to the highway that continued into the valley where the tiny hamlet of La Riviere was situated.

Across this gravel road, in sight of their farm was the little one room school house, with its pot-bellied stove, that the young Morleys attended. Later in life, they would attend the high school in the little hamlet of La Riviere, barely one mile away from the top of the prairies.

The English speaking residents of the town of La Riviere had a strange peculiarity. They couldn't pronounce the name of their own town. Most simply refused to struggle with an easternized naming of their resident hamlet, so, they anglicized the pronunciation of the name of their town by combining La with Riviere as one single word ... Lar-rivi-aire and shortened it further to just Larv-yer.

During the fall harvest, other members of the Morley clan from neighbouring farms would gather to help each other bring in the grain from the various fields. Each family owned close to a square section of land, that they had built their farms on and sowed it with different crops throughout the year. A square section of land was equivalent to one square mile or 2.56 square kilometres.

It was during the harvest that one's warmest memories lay. As the fields were swathed in rows extending over a mile, Willie J. would park his combine or tractor, shut off the engine at twelve o'clock noon, get off his machine, wipe his face with his neckerchief, and stand beside his machine and wait. The hot sun beat down relentlessly. There was just an edge of a cool breeze. The crackle of dragonfly wings filled the air. For the dragonflies ... lunch was a constant.

Mable and her children would then head out from the farmhouse with fruits, salads, ice cold jugs of orange drink and sandwiches. The family car would be driven across the open field to the silent machine where Willie J. stood. As the children spread a blanket out on the ground, Mable leaned up against Willie J, planted a kiss to his cheek as he lowered his face to meet hers...

"I brought your favourite."

She pointed to the carrot salad, a cool dessert on this hot day. Plates and utensils were laid out. For all practical purposes, it was just one big picnic ... a picnic to be played out every day for the month of harvesting. As everyone sat around on the blanket, Mable would pour water into a basin to allow Willie J. to wash his face and hands. The deep furrows of tan lines in his face were well weathered markers of years spent in the fields communing with Nature.

The picnic was part of the work day practised and duplicated on a daily basis by all who lived on these farms throughout Canada and all across North America. There was a sense of great belonging to similar families everywhere numbering in the tens of millions across the continent. Here was home ... here was freedom.

This particular Morley clan, of Mable and Willie J's, had inherited a strange gift from another century. Someone had placed an old railroad caboose on the land down alongside the slough sometime back in the 1880s before the CPR [Canadian Pacific Railroad] was even an entity. It seemed to have no wheels and was most probably placed there by hunters using it as a hut for one reason or another. Yet ... there was never any explanation regarding its true origins. It was there even before Willie J's father. His father and mother never talked about it other than that, it appeared one day down on their property. Even the CPR was interested in what they called an antique as it was different from any caboose of any railroad company that the CPR had ever seen.

It really stood out from the surrounding prairie. The reddish-brown paint had never peeled away despite the constant onslaught of summer rains, hail and winter storms. That was odd. Willie J. remembered one summer when Albert accidentally damaged the wood frame around the back door. The next day out at the caboose, the damage had been repaired but neither Albert nor Willie J. knew by whom it had been repaired. That too was extremely odd.

The inside of the caboose had aged but, not the outside. The old caboose out in the slough was empty. It was like a sentinel...serene. You could still go inside though and climb the fireman's pole to the second level. Life was hard, with long hours of physical labour under a hot sun in the summer, and feeding livestock and fowl in the desolate winters.

Willie and Mable had a daughter named Evelyn, the oldest child, and two sons, the eldest son Manfred and the youngest boy of their clan ... ten year old Eduard. These children were the immediate nephews and niece of Albert Morley. Albert was Willie's closest brother.

It was 1943. World War II was in full carnage. Even then, the war seemed almost remote. There was a disconnect. It was happening far away on the other side of the world. North America was still a tranquil place despite the old radio's nightly reports of European and Asian fighting. Chores still had to be done around the farm, the garden weeded and the old horse drawn buggy kept up for the drive into Larvyer for supplies, groceries and farm implements.

Eduard sometimes joined his father and his uncle Albert, Willie J's favourite brother, in the old scow when they fished off the lake. They often used the old caboose to flay their day's catch of grayling fish. But this year brought a draught to the area of southern Manitoba. The result was a bone dry slough. The moisture collected from winter was still held captive underneath the parched and cracked surface. Elsewhere, tall reeds nearly five feet high, blanketed the slough's surface everywhere with large bald surfaces showing through where the water table had all but evaporated.

The caboose still had windows intact and Eduard would sometimes reflect on how the light diffused warmly through those panes of glass. You could barely see out of them but you could make out the play of light, form and shadow. The caboose also had a lantern hanging from the rear door outside the caboose... the fuel ... long since evaporated ... the wick ... long since disintegrated. Now it was simply a non-functioning antique.

It was on a hot clear day in the month of July and ten year old Eduard was bathing his new black American cocker spaniel, Mickey, in a square metal tub, on the grass beside the house. The new puppy, barely six weeks old, tried to look over the edge of his metal bath tub. Eduard's dad too, had a dog ... a young pup about the same age as Mickey. It was an eight week old collie named Towzer. Eduard had the chore of looking after both, but to Eduard, it was a privilege. As he splashed Mickey with water, mom appeared around the corner of the house in an aproned dress.

Eduard loved her baked bread, the aroma of which now drifted out from the house. He had one more chore of the day before sitting down to six o'clock dinner. He needed, as she reminded him, to retrieve the mail from the mailbox a kilometre down the old dusty road. It saved the postman from travelling all the way up into the yard. It was a courtesy. In winter though, it could be a brutal two kilometre walk there and back.

Today, however, Eduard felt different. He felt something unusual about it. It was almost ... a premonition. Eduard had never felt like this before. It bothered him. He couldn't quite put his finger on it. He simply felt it. He looked out across the marshlands that he knew as the slough. He hesitated. There was something there ... he could sense it. He looked around the farmyard as if to catch a glimpse of a ghost hiding behind the corner of one of the grey barns.

Perhaps, Eduard thought, it was the uncanny stillness. There wasn't a breeze. He could always hear the flies in the porch on the screens. Now they were silent. Huh. He laughed inside at himself.

Looking down at the metal tub, he could see that even Mickey was frozen, attentive, as if the puppy could pick up on the strange quiet. Eduard looked around one last time, slowly scanning the horizon, then shaking the silliness off, he concentrated on getting this last chore over and done with. Eduard dried Mickey off and brought him into the porch of the house. The porch had no windows save a wrap around screen that was boarded up during the long winter months.

In his suspenders and rolled up sleeves, Eduard wheeled his bicycle out into the farm yard, through the gate and was now pedaling down the dirt road with the farmhouse receding behind him. He headed towards the gravelled municipal road. On his right a yellow field of oats crackled with the sounds of huge blue dragonflies ravenously devouring other helpless insects on the wing. They were the apex insect predators on his parents' farm. He stopped by the field of oats and husked a few seeds from one of the stocks. He put them in his mouth, wetting them while chewing. He found out from his dad that you could chew the oats like gum and he mimicked the old man now, as if chewing tobacco but without the spit. He had left his bike on the road for a few minutes as he walked into the tall strands of grain to husk a few more seeds.

Just then, a rather large sapphire blue dragonfly landed on his hand. The loud noise of the crackling beating wings took him by complete surprise. He yelled while trying to fling the monster off his hand. The blue dragonfly was like a giant spider with wings. Its hold was tenacious. It might have bitten him if he hadn't clawed it off. He shuddered recalling the stories he was told of prehistoric dragon flies with wingspans nearly a metre across. On his left side, the land was pasture. It stretched down to the slough. His father was helping his older brother Manfred build a farm on the other side of this water shed.

Since the slough this year was bone dry, which didn't happen often, it was possible to cross on foot to the other side. Manfred was to inherit that other farm. Along that side of the dirt road, leading away from the farm house, upon which he was now riding, a row of telephone posts nearly twenty feet high carried wires that transported the power to connect their phone to the outside world. Sometimes, when the wind swept across the prairies, the wires would reverberate like the sound of waves rushing upon a distant shore.

Eduard reached the last telephone-pole on which their family mailbox was nailed. It had the initials W. J. Morley stenciled onto it. He opened the lid. It creaked. Eduard retrieved the three letters and stuffed them into his shirt and let the tin lid of the mailbox drop with a metallic bang. The sound woke him to another realization.

The frogs always croaked loudly in the ditches on either side of the municipal gravel road that swept pass the dirt road leading back up to the farm house. But, at that moment... they were strangely silent. Eduard turned his bicycle around to begin the journey back up to the house. He hadn't pedaled far ... maybe fifty feet ... when something odd grabbed his attention. The crackling of dragon fly wings was no longer audible.

The air was still.

No sound.

There was that chill up his spine again. He hated himself for doing so but he stopped pedaling and put his left foot firmly on the ground. He listened intently. He looked across the field of oats. He could see the red combine his father had been driving. It was sitting still. He could barely make out his father walking across the vast yellow wilderness. From that distance, his father was a tiny stick of a shadow. It reassured him. He wasn't alone out here. He was after all, one of the guys. Guys weren't scared to walk alone.

Suddenly, it became uncomfortably clear, that as his father in the far distance headed ever closer to the farm house, Eduard could sense that there was something else out here with him. Fear hit him squarely in the chest. Heart pounding, he snapped his head to the right scanning the emptiness across the slough. It was as though something out there was watching his every move, a feeling he could not shake. His breathing was deeper and faster. In the few moments that were to follow, out there on the lonely prairies, there would be an event that would present itself to the young Eduard ... an event so strange that it would affect him for the rest of his life.

It was then, imperceptible at first, that he had noticed the dust just slightly rise from all over the slough. It was circulating counter-clockwise. It rose a few feet off the ground. Then ... as it gradually picked up its rotational cycle around the slough, it rose majestically some five hundred maybe six hundred feet in the air. It appeared to resemble a super whirl-wind or giant dust devil and it was a staggering three thousand feet across. It was a behemoth.

The sun's reflection cut across it in dazzling rainbow colours. But there wasn't a cloud in the sky. The metal basket on the front of his bike began to clatter. He could feel the coins in his pocket pull on his pants, away from his leg. Willie J. had already reached the courtyard and was making his way through the oak trees surrounding it. It blinded his field of vision from happenings outside the farmyard.

No sound.

Eduard could still not hear the frogs in the ditches. He was mesmerized ... all the more so because of its terrifying strangeness. Then, something electrifying sliced into his psyche like a hot knife through butter. He could see it through the dusty walls of this colossal whirlwind. It was on the back of the caboose. He could scarcely believe what he was seeing. It was the antique lantern at the rear of the caboose.

The lantern was lit with a bright yellowish-orange glow.

Still .... no sound.

Eduard could make out the luminescence of what he thought were millions of fireflies. But it wasn't. It was a strange static electricity crackling silently within the behemoth. The aurora of multi-coloured light dancing above the giant began to fade to a pale green. The strange aurora blinked out. Then the dazzling giant of a dust devil collapsed back onto the ground leaving only tendrils of its former presence like a patchwork of dusty clouds lying helter-skelter over the slough.

But the lantern was still lit. It shone like a fiery orange beacon through those dusty clouds. It almost seemed to be trying to get his undivided attention ... which it apparently already had. The light wasn't playing off the dirty stained glass anymore, as he once thought. It glowed ever brighter and finally, in a flash that was more likened to a high intensity explosion of light ... seared its way through the caboose, and blasted out through the railcar's windows with such intensity, that the young Eduard had to look momentarily away.

Then... like a hammer to the chest ... it was out. Just like that. This terrified him even more. His eyes were wide open. His jaw was slack. He could make out no one in or around the caboose.
The clattering of his bicycle basket stopped. The coins fell back down in the pockets of his pants. Something had just happened out there on the slough and he didn't want to have any part of it. He had seen big dust devils before but this ... this ... to his young mind was something very different.

A slight breeze wafted over the fields once again. Frogs were croaking for mates in the ditches. The crackles of dragonfly wings were once again audible. Eduard saw that his left hand had an iron grip on the handlebars. His right hand seemed unusually light weight. He brought it up to his face. It was shaking uncontrollably. It took three or four tries to get his damn foot back onto the bicycle pedal ... he was trembling so much.

He was on his bike again ... a little wobbly perhaps ... but racing for all he was worth to get to the farm house ... his safe haven ... when he heard his name being called out from a great distance ...coming from across the slough. It so surprised him that, he stopped pedaling as soon as he reached the gate to the farmyard by putting both feet on the dusty ground, bringing him to a dead stop, panting heavily, jaw flexed open ... and turned ... to once more scan the great expanse that was the slough.

Eduard held his breath as he tried to focus all his senses on his surroundings. There was an eerie whistle from the light wind as it wrapped itself across the telegraph wires. The tops of the reeds half a mile away were being gently caressed by the wind as it blew across the slough. He thought he was going mad. There was no one there.

STORIES of the VANISHED

It had been some three weeks since that incident out in the fields back in July. Eduard never mentioned it to his parents. He was too immersed in the day to day life of his family and friends and chores in and around the farm. Canadian football was now Eduard's passion. But the event was brought back to him every time he went down that dusty road to collect the mail. He saw no evidence of it happening again, so the event slid ever further back into his memories. Eventually, the memory of that day became a lost event. It had nearly faded away completely.

It was 1953. Ten years had passed. Eduard was twenty and long since graduated from the school in Larvyer. He was working as a Station Master for the CPR [Canadian Pacific Railroad] as it was known. Eduard's other passion was trains. He passed this passion onto his oldest and first nephew... Daniel. Whenever Eduard visited the small metropolitan city of Winnipeg during Christmas, he would take his nephew to the Hudson's Bay store. He and his nephew would head upstairs to Toy Land to immerse themselves fully in everything that had to do with the wonderful world of trains. Eduard would spend long hours teaching this nephew how to draw trains whenever his nephew visited him, on the Morley farm, during the long summers.

Eduard's one and only sister Evelyn had for nine years been married into another clan, the McIntyres' Her family consisted of three small boys ... Daniel nine, a tall lanky light blue eyed boy, pale complexion, quite skinny, slightly freckled, fine boned, high cheek bones, straight auburn hair and slightly buck toothed. Even his ears protruded just slightly out from the sides of his head. Then there was Benedict or just Benny for short, who was shorter at about eight years of age, slightly stocky even pudgy and always the jovial one of Evelyn's siblings. He had even acquired an early taste and appreciation for money. Finally there was Gordon, barely six, shorter than Benny with a skinny build, high plump cheeks, brown hair and eyes with a penchant for getting into mischief and fights.

Eduard's older brother Manfred had also recently married his high school sweetheart Gardenia who, together, reared a son, eight year old Devin, stocky build with a medium tan complexion, strong, brown hair and hazel eyes along with a five year old little girl named Dianne. Dianne, ever so cute with her platinum blonde hair, tiny pigtails done up in red ribbon, in a little white dress became inseparable from her brother.

Gathered around the small kitchen table were Eduard, Willie J., his wife Mable, Evelyn and her husband W. Rolf McIntyre, a sales man, with their three sons Daniel, Benny and Gordon. It was there that Eduard opened up a new dialogue rarely discussed among family members. Eduard wanted to know whether the stories surrounding that caboose out on the edge of the slough were true. He wanted to know more. Evelyn had heard about those stories as well and looked across into the eyes of her mother. Mable looked across at Willie J. relaxed, smoking a cigar by the kitchen window in his favourite chair. He didn't look up at the family crew husking corn which they had earlier brought in from the garden a couple of hours ago.

Willie J. put down his newspaper, took another drag on his cigar, leaned back and began slowly to collect his thoughts before he spoke.

"What do you want to know about it son?"

Eduard asked him bluntly "Heard it simply appeared out of nowhere. No one knows of the story behind it. Why is that Dad?"

So, Willie began… "Even your grandfather and his father before him don't know. Not even the CPR. No one knows how that old caboose got where it is today. Some say she was built there. Don't believe it. The wheels are still on that thing."

Eduard was astounded. "The wheels are still on it? You have to be kidding. It's sitting on the undercarriage."

Before Eduard could say more, old Willie interjected...

"Albert and I checked it out some twenty-five years or so ago. We took a spade to it. And you know what we found? The iron wheels were sitting on some type of metal. Probably rails under it still. Imagine. Somebody even had it placed on rails. How's that for strange?" Old Willie J. chuckled, hesitated for a moment as if to contemplate what he had just revealed to the family, and then, shook his head and got back to his paper.

Rolf looked at Eduard...

"Why would anybody put it on rails?"

Eduard sat back from the kitchen table in disbelief with his head cocked to one side.

Mable then spoke up ... looking at Willie J. "You remember Willie what you told me about what your dad said to you about the caboose many, many years ago?

Without looking up from his paper, old Willie softly intoned...

"Yes. There is something else."

Old Willie looked down at the floor to collect his thoughts.

"My dad once told me that the caboose once stood in the northwest section of the slough. Today, it stands in the southwest section. Its been moved. I suspect that we have a caboose that circumnavigates the slough every so often. I remember it in various positions over the years but always thought it was the action of a sort of permafrost ... you know ... melting, run-off, drying and heaving of that marsh crust. That's when Albert and I decided one fine day to check it out."

Deep down, Willie knew that didn't sound quite right. But, it was nothing to get stirred up over. Mable interjected once again.

"Tell them about that easterner and his three companions who were up here. No harm in telling it now ... right?'

It was Evelyn's turn.

"What easterners?"

Then Evelyn remembered. She was eleven years old. It was around 1933. She remembered the kindly gentleman and his three younger companions... "Batt" Menzie who hailed from the little town of Souris and later retired to Larvyer, and his two friends, a switchmen named Don McManus and the other, a train conductor. They all took a special interest in that ancient railcar in the slough.

Back in the 1930s, during the Dust Bowl, an easterner who was an American by name of Charlie Stensis, working for the National Museum of Canada [NMC] had crossed the prairies looking for ancient fossil marine dragons. He had found them on an escarpment barely three km just outside the small hamlet of Miami, Manitoba. It caused a sensation in and around that area of the Bible belt. Stensis was aware of a small lake where both duck hunting and fishing were quite good. It was the future Lake Morley. It was that year that the slough had gained its legendary notoriety. They had contacted the previous Morley land owner for permission to hunt on the slough. It was Albert who had offered to take them out that day.

During their day hunting at the slough, Charlie Stensis returned to Larvyer for the day's supplies. Albert, for his part, helped the three contract employees of Stensis' to set up blinds on the lake using the old scow of a row boat. They decided to place the blinds near the green and white coloured derelict caboose where they would sit down for a tea and lunch. For three of them, it was to be their last. Stensis' three contract employees were well known in the vicinity.

William "Batt" Menzie and his wife Janet lived in Larvyer. Batt was a Conductor for CP Rail. He played once for the NHL [National Hockey League in Canada]. He was physically fit. His other pursuit was arrowheads and other aboriginal antiquities. He was also an excellent trapper.

Batt's two companions were Switchman and Conductor ... also for the CPR. Don was a lapidarist/ amateur geologist and the other fine fellow a gemologist. The association of these Larvyer residents was obvious. Their association with dinosaur hunter Charlie Stensis was expected. They were all intrepid explorers and knew the quarries within fifty miles around the town.

Charlie had returned from his shopping spree in Larvyer. He parked the car on the municipal road beside the ditch adjacent to the tiny lake. They had bought their main supplies from the big town of Morden to dig out some of the marine dragons of the Pembina Escarpment overlooking the prairies below. Their chosen spot was an area known locally as the Twin Sister Buttes located centrally in a little dished out desert badlands on the top of the escarpment. At night, Charlie's crew would sit atop those buttes and spend the night star-gazing.

The supplies from Larvyer consisted mostly of spices and some food and drink from the town's only grocery store owned by the McConnell's. Little boxes of coloured popcorn and boxes of crackerjacks supplied the sweet tooth. It was, after all, the 1930s.

Daniel was nearly five and astounded that his family was talking about dragons as though they had actually existed. He still hadn't a clue about the ancient history of the world he was born into. This was exciting to him. He had never known of the existence of any other world but the one that presently surrounded him.

Kellogg's cereal manufacturer was poised to place the first toys of prehistoric animals in its Rice Krispies boxes. This was soon to open entire new vistas of imagination for North American children. It would be the defining factor that would lead Daniel into a new lifelong passion that would influence the rest of his life. Some dark nights he was left alone with his Kellogg's cereal Rice Krispy dinosaur toys on the big dining table in the living room of the old farm. His first thoughts of evolutionary change were beginning to take hold.

Lightning would flash outside, bringing him nose to window to peer out across the darkened garden, watching the shapes of the oak tree trunks flash in the light of the storms. It reminded him of a herd of long necked brontosaurs.

Farm life was isolating but its bleakness and massive vistas surely stirred the imagination. Sometimes as a child, he would venture down to the giant slough to glimpse the wild life and discover small fish hugging its shore line. Each day he would venture down there, he would notice that the fish were growing, abandoning their fins for legs, fish tails for no tails, gills for lungs then, hopping up on land as fully terrestrial tetrapods ... amphibians. These were the creatures that lived the first part of their life as fish and the second part of their life as land animals. Those particular amphibians were known as frogs. Nature was teaching this young child a very different view of creation ... one that would put him on a very different path than the rest of his kin folk.

His two brothers however, would find different paths but, together, all three would be forcibly thrown into a realm that none of them were prepared for. This was later, in the 1950s.

Returning back into the 1930s, Stensis and his crew fished and hunted 'til early evening. The catch was brought into the caboose. The old scow was tied up on the landing and all four men sat comfortably in the interior of that caboose preparing the mallards and two fish that Albert caught. The ancient Coleman stoves heated the interior pleasantly. The metal plates and cutlery were set out and the tea was boiled. Altogether a very pleasant evening with discussion of their days "catch", in the Pembina Hills, of a mosasaur ... a seventeen foot specimen of a marine dragon called Clidastes. This marine dragon was to be crated and sent back east to Ottawa.

After the meal, it was time to get back to their encampment in the Pembina Hills outside the little hamlet of Miami. Charlie left once again for the one mile descent into the valley to Larvyer. He was to make a phone call to Ottawa. The crew was to clean up and be ready for the trip back into the Pembina Hills. Albert untied the old scow from the caboose and began to row to the opposite side of the 1 km wide lake to where he had left the horse and buggy. He reached his destination, tied up the scow then walked the ten meters to his buggy to retrieve some maps and then got ready to head back to the caboose.

As the three men packed up their gear and stepped out of the rear of the caboose, they hesitated.

"Odd..." Albert thought ... the horses were spooked.

Could there be a cougar nearby?

Damn. He was unarmed. The other guys had the shotguns but he didn't think to bring his.

Then, the event presented itself.

A fog, in the form of a spectacular whirl wind came up unexpectedly and completely enveloped the slough. Albert turned and watched in amazement. It lifted and began to swirl counter-clockwise as it arched slowly, gently inward. He had never experienced anything like it ... not in his entire life. He didn't know whether to stay and witness this event or just plain run from it. It was truly frightening. He turned, squinting his eyes.

"Strange. No sound."

Just then, something utterly unheard of made its grand entrance in the middle of the night. High overhead of the swirling fog was a magnificent aura of light not unlike the aurora borealis. The colours were spectacular as they danced to and fro, waving, like a gigantic veil of reds, greens and yellows. There was a strange sparkle of electrical static. Then it faded into a monochromatic veil of green lights and blinked out. When the once swirling fog had silently collapsed back into the marsh and completely dissipated, Albert could not see the light from the lanterns of his compatriots, inside the caboose.

The ancient lantern on the outside however was miraculously burning and then... suddenly...a brilliant flash of light seared its way through the stained windows of the caboose and blasted its way out through the remnants of the fog ... nearly lighting up the entire slough ... and went out. But how was that even possible? He stood there, eyes frozen upon the caboose. He waited for what seemed half a minute. There was no movement in or out of the caboose. Where were the guys? Albert's heart was pounding. He turned around and climbed into the buggy and brought it up on top of the dirt road, the municipal road that was to be gravelled in the near future.

He arrived at the caboose only minutes later. Albert secured the reigns before getting out of the buggy and lowered himself to the ground. He slowly turned around to face the caboose. He froze. There was no one there. He listened intently. Nothing made a sound. Nothing moved. The railcar simply stood there ... in the centre of nowhere, staring back from the immensity of the slough. He took a deep breath.

"Where the hell did they go?" Albert thought.

There was nothing but prairie for a mile in every direction.

"Could they still be in the rail car? Was this some kind of childish game ... a prank on him? They didn't seem to be the type. What the hell was going on?"

It was then that Charlie Stensis' vehicle climbed up from the dusty road, just over the hill from Larvyer to the flat prairie above and into Albert's view.

Charlie parked his vehicle just behind Albert's buggy, on the opposite side of the road, then slipped out of the driver's seat and walked over to Albert. Albert was just standing there looking back at him with a strange expression of bewilderment on his face. His hands were outstretched to his sides as if asking a question. He didn't know what to say. He had no explanation. They both went back to the rail car half expecting the "joke" to air. It didn't.

They both climbed onto the two platforms from opposite ends of the rail car. They slowly opened both doors. Both men could see one another at opposite ends of the rail car in the fading light. Neither one moved. Their eyes scanned the interior. Not even the kitchen equipment was left in there. They both turned to peer across the surrounding area outside the rail car. At first Charlie was angered at this being a stupid joke of sorts but it didn't seem right somehow. They decided to walk the dusty roads in opposite directions from each other to see if they could find the missing men. They were hard workers. They wouldn't have just picked up and walked away in the middle of nowhere. It made no sense.

By the following day, the families of the missing men were deeply concerned that some type of foul play was at hand. The only police agent in town called in for help from the then small metropolitan city of Winnipeg. It became big news as the mystery intensified. They had simply vanished. Albert's explanation shed no light as to the circumstances just before the vanishing act. He was subsequently shunned and became somewhat of a social outcast. There was a deeply held suspicion that Albert was somehow involved in their disappearance. Willie J. stood fast with his brother. It wasn't like Albert to lie. They often fished together for many years. Willie J. knew his brother better than anyone.

Willie's family were his only contacts. He never married and tended to live alone which deepened suspicion. He was always invited to holiday dinners but always remained aloof. Mable didn't like him around but included Albert because of her husband Willie Js. relationship with him and Albert knew it. She was resigned to put up with it. What else could she do? Albert was still family.

Willie J. did not mention that last part about Albert and the event as he finished the story to his family gathered in the small kitchen. Eduard sat motionless as he heard the story. No wonder Uncle Albert never talked about it. Even Eduard's own mom and dad never told him. But Eduard now was having another revelation of his own. The memory of that incident ten years ago was back like a frightening dark cloak clad vampire standing in the doorway. Why did he have to go and bring that subject up?

For Eduard, it had unfortunately brought that incident closer to reality than he had ever anticipated. He almost felt that he had to get off the farm. He was now glad that Manfred was inheriting the new farm, for what was for him, on the other side of that slough, a potential nightmare waiting to be re-released. He wanted no part of it, yet, he already was. He couldn't say anything to anybody. They would think he had been out in the sun or worse. His mother would come down on him like a ton of bricks for even suggesting that Albert's story held any merit. Eduard was even afraid to tell Albert lest Albert slip in conversation that he wasn't the only witness in the family to the event.

No. No. This had to be kept to himself. What about the danger to the rest of the family? He must make sure that Evelyn and Rolf's kids, his little nephews were never allowed to go down to this strange, unfathomable marsh alone. Hell. He wasn't even going to go down there himself. He'll be damned if he was going to allow anyone else. But it rang hollow. How could he protect anyone with 100% assurance? He knew, deep down, he couldn't. But he remained resolute about telling anyone else. That, as he was to find out many years later, was a disastrous mistake he would regret for a very long time.

Eduard left the kitchen and took Mickey with him for a walk around the dusty road surrounding the courtyard. He had to think this through. Evelyn cleared the table for dinner while Mable went to the potbelly stove to fire up a few logs for tea. After dinner, Evelyn and her mother stacked the dishes on the old white tiled counter top by the porcelain sink. Water was boiling in a metal pot on the pot bellied stove that was used to fill the kitchen sink to wash dishes in. Eduard had returned at dusk from his walk with Benny and Daniel in tow. He grabbed his football and took all Evelyn's kids out to the farmyard for a game of football. It was tradition and they were all happy to do it. The farm- yard was lit by a single powerful yard light. It reminded everyone of the lights that shone over a football stadium.

UNCLE ALBERT

That same summer, Eduard took the boys over to the Morley farm that was "Uncle Albert's". People rarely visited Uncle Albert save his sister Aunt Lilith and his brother Willie J. This day, it was a dark gray sky. Cool. It threatened rain. The inside of Albert's house was strange indeed. There were clocks everywhere. The din of ticking clocks was astonishing. It was Albert's passion. It reminded him of how every moment of time was precious even when sleeping. He had a book shelf, a veritable library on geology, biology and clocks. Daniel loved the place. Benny thought it was amusing if not down right weird. Gordon was simply mesmerized. He was touching everything. Eduard caught Gordon out of the corner of his eye. With a loud whisper directed toward Gordon, Eduard barked...

"Don't touch!! Leave that alone!!"

The boys busied themselves with play outside the house. There was something on Eduard's mind that he wished to relay to Albert. After about an hour, Eduard came out and asked Daniel if he wanted to stay a while. Daniel nodded affirmatively. It was because Uncle Albert knew something about dinosaurs, that Daniel wanted to hang back. It was Uncle Albert's collection of books on geology and biology that told Daniel that here was somebody he could talk to. His brothers and his uncle Eduard were planning to be back from Larvyer in about an hour. Eduard asked Daniel what he wanted in the form of sweets from the general store there. As the car left Albert's yard, Daniel went back indoors to get better acquainted with his other uncle.

Albert was a large stocky man. In fact, Albert was more like a Santa Claus without a beard. Everyone knew Albert was eccentric. But no one knew just how eccentric. Daniel wanted to stay with Uncle Albert to try and get to know him a little better. And that did happen in a way that Daniel was unprepared for. Albert made a little lunch with tea for the both of them.

"So Daniel..." Albert began...

"What would you like to know about dinosaurs?" Daniel had only a small collection of toy dinosaurs and some children's books on them.

"Everything, Uncle Albert."

Albert tilted his head at Daniel and paused... "Everything now... would you? That's a tall order."

Albert took a deep breath... "Alright, we'll start with their classification in the Linnaean sense." He told Daniel how all creatures got two names...a binomial designation, a genus, and species if you like. After a brief introduction bearing on the phylogenetic classification of dinosaurs, the subject abruptly intensified.

"I'll tell you something very astounding Daniel. You know those chickens on your grandpa's farm? Well. Those are dinosaurs. Dinosaurs were feathered...Daniel. The birds we know today are the only dinosaurs that we have left in the world after that cataclysmic extinction event."

Albert waited for a response from Daniel.

"Could Uncle Albert be drunk?" Daniel thought.

He didn't seem to be.

"How do you know this Uncle Albert?" Daniel asked.

Albert's face lost that soft smile. It became more stern… almost a frown. Henry got up from the table with his cup of tea in hand and walked over to the kitchen window. He said nothing for about fifteen seconds, as if pondering something better left unsaid.

"I was there … nearly ten years ago when your Uncle Eduard was only a ten year old boy" ... Albert quietly intimated.

"What do you mean Uncle Albert?" As frightened as Daniel was becoming, he was quietly fascinated by Uncle Albert's revelation.

"Would you like to see them for yourself?"

Daniel didn't know how to answer. "Oh ....kay..." he said quietly, unsure of what Uncle Albert meant. But Daniel was intrigued. Perhaps his uncle was to offer him a revelation about these great dragons ... but feathered? And alive today? This was almost too much, but his uncle didn't seem to be joking.

"Then meet me down by your grandpa's old slough." He turned and looked at Daniel as if waiting for a response.

"...When?" Daniel intoned.

Albert looked across at Daniel ... "Day after tomorrow ... nine o' clock in the morning ... and Daniel ... can you keep a secret?" Daniel nodded.

Albert reached up to his top book shelf and slid a binder out, swollen with notes ... field observations. He turned to Daniel.

"When I was a young man of about thirty, I saw a monster sized dust devil ...the likes of which no man has ever seen. I was in the caboose. I was having tea with my lunch. I was with your grandfather. We forgot to bring a little snifter of whiskey." Albert smiled. "So your grandpa went back to the farmhouse to retrieve it. He never knew I had taken the trip. I can take you on that same trip. I worked it out that every twenty years precisely on the eighth of July every summer, Nature opens up in all its glory for you to explore right here ... in this very marshland."

Albert turned and looked out the window once again. He paused...

"It's a place where dreams and nightmares rush together."

Albert took a deep breath.

"This place is the most unique in all of creation Daniel."

Uncle Albert paused in reflection for some time after, ever looking out the window, watching images glide through his mind, like ghostly ships on a distant ocean. For Daniel, that was a pretty cryptic message but, he was just an eleven year old boy and Uncle Albert was quickly becoming the most exciting family relation he had ever known. Okay, so he was a little eccentric ... even strange ... with all that clockwork going on in his farmhouse. He lived alone, so he probably talks to himself. Maybe a few marbles were rolling around loose, but so what? He was a great story teller. And he had this strange interest in dinosaurs. Daniel was sold on his Uncle Albert. Together they were just going to sit in the caboose and drink tea while Daniel would listen to his uncle's stories. He just had to bring his two brothers.

Albert continued…

"There were many cold mornings when a little splash of whiskey in our tea took the edge off the chill. We put a little pot-belly stove in that caboose and piled a little firewood up beside it."

Albert's eyes almost watered. "Long conversations…"

He caught Daniel's intense stare... studying him. "You know... old timers talking about old times" ... his uncle said light heartedly, with an awkward smile.

Daniel broke his intense stare... "Oh."

"We're going on a dinosaur hunt down by the old slough Daniel. Bring your brothers if they want to come. I'll bring along some spears and a couple of bows and arrows. I'll phone your grandpa tonight. The old slough's pretty dry this year so we'll be able to hunt them in the tall reeds. Of course, Daniel thought,

"Uncle Albert's talking about hunting birds while pretending they were dinosaurs. That'll be great fun."

Mable was not pleased. She didn't like the idea of her daughter's boys alone with Albert. Willie sighed as he rolled his eyes.

"Albert may be a bit eccentric Mable but... he's not crazy."

Mable whirled around from the kitchen sink...

"No! They're not going and that's it! I don't want to speak of this anymore..."she whispered intensely as Eduard came in through the porch door. Willie's eyes met Eduard's as he quickly intimated, throwing a couple of glances over at Mable.

Eduard understood and interjected... "I'll take them down and stay with Albert".

If looks could kill, Mable turned sharply to Willie and then to Eduard and back to the sink.

"Do what you like but don't let those boys out of your sight!" She turned to Eduard...glaring.

Eduard put both hands up...

"Okay, okay mom." He looked at his dad and rolled his eyes.

Mable with her back turned away, hunched over the sink washing dishes murmured...

"I saw that."

Willie winked at Eduard and softly said... "She don't miss a thing."

"I'll wash up mom and give you a hand in a minute in setting the dining room table." Eduard shot back.

"Put out the extra sheaves. Place them in the table..." Mable instructed. The wooden sheaves (planks) had the effect of lengthening the darkly stained dining room table.

"We're having guests over tonight."

"Who's coming mom?"

"Manfred and Gardenia's two kids, Bill and Dorothy's three kids as well as Deanna and Steven's daughter Beverly" Mable called out. "Your Uncle Charlie and Auntie Cynthia will be here as well. So you have nine little ones to look after Eduard."

Eduard sighed.

"I didn't hear that..." Mable uttered.

Eduard called back... "It'll be fine mom."

INTO THE STORM

It was the second of July, 1955. Manfred and Gardenia were occupying their new farm on the other side of the slough. In the summers, their son and daughter, Devin and Dianne often came over for a visit.

Manfred and Gardenia brought over their son and daughter, and for once, even their farm dog... Skipper. Manfred and Gardenia were heading out to Pilot Mound to attend a wedding and then drive eleven hundred miles to Alberta to visit friends for some ten days.

. . .

Skipper was a very protective dog at home, in his territory but, not here. Here he had to contend with the incumbents, Mickey and Towzer. Skipper was unusually intimidated and begged to stay in the car. At best, it wasn't pleasant for him. He wanted badly to go home and the incessant whining and tail between the legs let everybody know. Worse, Skipper also had a bad run in with turkeys. Willie and Mable's farm were alive with these feathered demons. After several visits with Skipper in tow, Mickey and Towzer only reluctantly accepted the old intruder. Manfred and Gardenia were trying to get all three dogs acquainted, in a more positive manner. It was trying.

That night, after dinner, the six boys played football with Eduard and Gabriel, Eduard's distant cousin, while the girls helped Mable clean up the dinner dishes before retiring upstairs to sleep. It was a three room upstairs compartment. One room served as the toilet room, the other for Dianne, Vera and Beverly with Mable, while the last bedroom, Eduard's bedroom, was reserved for the six boys.

Everyone had to contend with crickets in and out of the beds. They were everywhere. Their chirping made for an interesting night's sleep. But tonight, the boys had other plans. As soon as Eduard closed their bedroom door, and he had gone downstairs to join with his father Willie J. and Gabriel, the boys upstairs made their move. It was a dark, pitch black night with a warm breeze gently buffeting the tall evergreens. No clouds were visible to shield the star studded sky. It was a perfect evening.

Quietly, one by one, in their pyjamas, they stole silently out of bed and made their way through the window onto the porch roof below them. From there, they boosted each other up and onto the roof of the old house and quietly made their way to the summit. Once there, they straddled their legs across both sides of the roof. They leaned back and looked directly up into the blackest of nights. It was studded with stars.

My god, the stars.

One could easily see the Orion Nebula splashed across the night sky. It took their collective breath away. Silence reigned supreme if only for a few minutes as each boy collected his thoughts. The odd bat flittered by, which the boys mistook for birds.

It was two days since Daniel's visit with Uncle Albert.

Today was the day. Mable was always the first one up, braving the cold linoleum floor. She had the pot bellied stove going in no time after throwing on some logs. The floors of the house warmed quickly.

Breakfast was next. Everyone was downstairs at the kitchen table. After breakfast, there was work to do and the nine kids were left to themselves. Playing in the courtyard, Daniel wondered about the opportunity of seeing Uncle Albert. A plan was hatched. The nine kids walked down the groves of evergreens lining one side of the vegetable garden. They chose one of the trees, looked around to see if anybody was paying attention to them, and commenced a perilous climb up one of the sixty foot tall evergreens. The tops were swaying in the warm gentle breeze. Crows were screeching loudly. Mickey, Towzer and Skipper gathered by the base of the tree and whined their disapproval of being left behind. In less than eight minutes, Daniel, Devin, Beverly and Jacob had reached the summit. Bennie, Georgi and Dianne were on the next branches below them. Gordon and Vera were hanging on under them. One could see for miles in every direction. It was grand. Magnificent. There was back and forth banter from the kids on the lower branches. There was only silence from the kids at the trees summit as they quietly took in the enormous panoramic vista.

It was near half past eight. They had to be down at the slough by nine.

From the top of the swaying evergreen, the children could make out Uncle Albert's old pick-up truck. He was already there. Eduard was calling 'Where the hell are you guys? I'm going to leave without you! Do ya hear? Where are you?"

The climb down the evergreen was arduous at best. Daniel called out that they were coming. Could they make it down in time without alerting suspicion? Can't let anyone know we're up here. Daniel was the last to jump out of the tree at its base.

"Hah! No one's going to know we were up there" Daniel murmured to himself. As he stood up, his Uncle Eduard was standing right in front of him.

"Crap!" was the only word that came immediately to Daniel's mind.

"We'll talk about this later. Get in the truck guys ... NOW!" Eduard commanded.

They piled in. The dust cloud rose behind Eduard's truck as it sprinted down the old road advertising to Albert that they were on their way. Gabriel sat in the front with Eduard.

The kids sat in the open box.

Eduard's talk with Albert alerted him to a possible eighth of July "event". Much to Albert's relief, Eduard had told him about his sighting only twelve years ago. The date made Eduard uneasy. But if Albert was right, no one had to worry for another eight years. Eduard knew that Albert had been on some weird trip and suggested that he get a medical. Albert brushed it aside. It wouldn't make any difference to Albert now. He was aware that Eduard was far from convinced that he, Albert, was playing with a full deck. The trust only went so far. It was a lot for Albert to put on Eduard. But the six boys and three girls were more open.

Albert never showed Eduard his diary. He would explain to Eduard when he got there that it was a book of story telling ... fiction. But it wasn't. For Albert, it was something terrifying he experienced in life. But today, he was relaxed and was simply going to have fun with it all. He caught sight of Eduard's pickup churning up the dust as it headed away from the farm.

The pickup had now just arrived. Eduard set the hand-brake. The children got out of the back of the pick-up and rushed over to see their Uncle Albert in the caboose. Eduard looked up. The sky was partly cloudy but the horizon was a dark menacing purple. This outing wasn't going to last long. It'll be a good memory for the kids though. The wind was still, as Eduard took one last look around before entering the old caboose.

Mickey, Towzer and Skipper were left to play outside. He tied each dog to the rear platform of the caboose, outside, with enough leash to allow them to wander about. Albert already had the kids gathered around him. He had lots of dinner utensils for eating with, and lots of food. Gabriel had brought some packages of beef jerky. The kids each had a piece to chew on. It focused their attention.

Albert already had a parcel open. This was going to be a great craft show. In the intervening two hours, he taught them how to make an arrow and a bow. He let each of them practise on the individual kits he had saved for them. Albert had brought along some fifty arrows wrapped tightly in cloth he had made for himself as well as three fine bows.

In the next hour, he taught them a short course on First Aid. It was all great fun. What happened next was quite neat. In one corner of the caboose, Albert showed the kids an entire group of signatures that had been carved into the wooden wall of the caboose with the year carved in as well with the person's name. His grandfather had started the whole signature scratch-in tradition. Everyone took turns doing the same. Now there were nine new signatures with the new dates scratched in after them.

Eduard thought Albert was doing the kids a great justice ... really taking good care of them, training them well. At the end of the lessons, Albert took his copy of the First Aid manual and shoved it into a drawer in the kitchen of the caboose. Gabriel took note. He thought Albert was all right, probably a hunter and fisherman at heart. Gabriel joined in as he poured himself a little spirit from Albert's flask. Next day, Albert told the kids, he would go over with them what they learned today.

"I'm going to leave the survival manual right here." Albert instructed.

"This manual is never to leave the caboose. Comprendre?" The kids all nodded in unison. He waved the manual at them...

"Next time, I'll show you how to use strips of wood just like a string to tie logs together in case you have to make a raft. I'll even show you how to make a tarpaulin to mount on the raft. Then we'll learn how to make a fire without matches."

Albert's gaze fell quickly to the floor.

"I made a tarpaulin some ten years ago." He tapped a bundle under the bench with his foot.

"It's all there if you should need it." Albert caught himself. Why would they need it? That's something he did when he was taken by the "event".

Albert had brought only six backpacks with him ... filled with survival gear. He gave one to each of the five oldest boys and one to Beverly. They won't really need it he thought. This was just a life lesson. He was looking forward to more days like this with his grand nephews and nieces. Vera, Dianne and Gordon were the youngest of the nine kids. They required a different approach. But they would remember this day as a fun filled day to look back upon in moments of quiet reminiscing. He didn't care what Mable thought. He was going to become, once again, a welcome part of his family. Damn the nonsense!

Eduard looked at his uncle." Where'd you get the push to make all this survival gear Albert?"

Albert returned the glance with a whimsical look on his face and raised eyebrow.

"Had to, Eduard, my life depended on this self-made survival gear many a times. I'm still here because this equipment saved my ass on more than one occasion."

Eduard didn't like where this was going.

Albert turned to the kids "Hungry, anyone?"

It was quarter after eleven. Everyone was hungry and the wind outside was picking up. The sky had darkened. There were flashes of lightning on the horizon and the sound of distant thunder. Everett had left immediately to make lunch and an orange powdered drink for their little crew and would grab some whiskey for Albert and himself. Eduard made them promise to stay put in the caboose no matter what. If it started to rain, they were to take the dogs inside with them.

Eduard took Daniel aside and sternly emphasized ... "Daniel, I'm counting on you. Keep the kids inside 'til I get back and if it rains, bring the dogs inside. Do that and I won't tell grandma where I caught you and the kids today...deal?"

Daniel nodded.

Hell, where were they going to go? The two farmhouses were always in sight. Fifteen minutes after Eduard left, the kids were setting the small table and spreading out the heavy comforters on the benches to sit on.

"Uncle Albert thinks about everything," Daniel thought.

The lanterns, both of them, were burning. There was now a lot more light inside the caboose. The stove had been lit by Uncle Albert, they were warm at least. The temperature outside had dropped considerably. The first few drops of rain were splattering loudly against the window panes of the caboose. The kids were becoming afraid. Gabriel saved everyone from panic by suggesting they go up the fireman's pole and watch for their Uncle Eduard's return or even watch the storm itself. Daniel and Georgi had taken the dogs up onto the landing.

Then, the deluge hurtled down upon them.

As if this weren't scary enough, it turned to hail, lots of hail. He peered through the rear windows of the caboose. The hailstones were crashing against the windows and walls of the caboose.

Uncle Albert assured everyone that this happened all the time. The dogs were gone. They had taken refuge under the landing. They should be safe there. They won't get wet. Albert suggested leaving them there.

No sooner had it started when the hail lifted. It even stopped raining. The sky was clearing. The dark clouds were slowly drifting towards the horizon still spitting flashes of light. The sun was beaming down again and rapidly drying everything off. By noon, Eduard was heading down the road again and out to the caboose. The dogs were back out sniffing the hail stones.

Eduard arrived and was concerned when he did not see the dogs. Daniel told Eduard that Uncle Albert thought the dogs were better underneath the railcar's rear carriage platform. Eduard thought for a moment. He let it go. Daniel was relieved.

After about one o'clock in the afternoon, the kids decided to head out and play. The cool breeze had returned. It was a little chilly. Eduard and Uncle Albert decided to spend some time together in the caboose, with Gabriel, drinking a bit of coffee flavoured with a shot of whiskey.

 By ten past three in the afternoon, the dark menacing clouds were on the distant horizon still spewing lightning some fifteen miles away. The kids were back in the caboose. Eduard had a phone call to make. Albert and Gabriel would stay here in the caboose with the kids 'til Eduard got back. It was to be only twenty minutes. Tomorrow, they would do some real hunting. Uncle Albert excused himself to go out to his truck to put the whiskey away, Gabriel followed.

He wanted to get to know this Uncle Albert of theirs a little better but Albert didn't know Gabriel well enough to confide in him about the "event". Perhaps in time, he might, but not now, not yet. Beverly, on the other hand, was excited to be with her cousins and gratified that her big brother, Gabriel, had turned up to join the little group. Gabriel wouldn't have missed being with his little sister for all the world.

The children began examining the bundle of arrows and the three bows along with the three spears. Uncle Albert had given them permission to examine them. They glanced around at each other. Wouldn't hurt to give it a trial run ... right? The backpacks were loaded. They put them on. Daniel, Devin and Jacob carefully strapped on the bows. They now looked like real hunters. Devin motioned for the rest of them to follow. Uncle Albert even brought wide rimmed hunter's hats for each of the nine kids.

This was pretty cool.

It came suddenly ... out of nowhere.

A freak lightning bolt out of the clear blue emanating from that distant storm arced across fifteen miles of open sky. It was huge and struck the distant shore of the marsh with a tremendous bang. Gabriel jumped and whirled around. He was thinking of the kids. Daniel felt the concussion as the sound wave hit them. It jarred them to the bone. Albert, shaken by the blast of sound and light, had dropped the whiskey flask on to the ground from his open truck door.

"What the ..." Albert looked around to see a column of thin smoke snake up from the marsh about a kilometre away.

"Wow"! Gabriel invoked as the two stood there together.

Both men had their attention riveted on the dark horizon.

"Must have been a freak bolt of lightning from quite a ways away. Had to be pretty powerful. You're never truly safe from that stuff" Albert warned.

Gabriel silently nodded. Albert bent down to get his whiskey flask. It had slid under the truck. He was chewing tobacco. He spat a brown gob onto the road. Gabriel winced.

In the dining room of the farmhouse, Eduard's phone went dead. He heard and felt the bang of the powerful bolt of lightning. Now he had to wind the hand device to reconnect again.

Unnoticed by everyone, a dust devil nearly three thousand feet across and covering the entire watershed had risen from the slough in a counter-clockwise direction. It was now ten feet high and rising rapidly. The rear door of the caboose was open. Six year old Gordon was standing on the landing outside.

Gordon was the first to notice ... "Hey! Guys! Come here! Look!"
Everyone rushed outside onto the landing where Gordon stood. The children all gathered by the rear door of the railcar and stood motionless not quite realizing what it was that they were looking at. The mountainous spiral had risen some five or six hundred feet into the air all around them. A rainbow of spectacular colors danced overhead and across the now dusty marsh. It was mesmerizing, enticing them off the platform of the railcar.

Albert was on his knees reaching for the bottle. "Gotcha." At that moment everything turned suddenly darker.

Gabriel called out to Albert "You gotta see this Albert".

Albert's heart was pounding. He slowly stood up and turned around, slack-jawed, dropping the flask at his feet which once again slid back under his truck. He didn't care.

He was leaning sharply into full panic mode.

"No ... no ... no ...no ...no ... it can't be happening! Oh my god no! Not again...it's not time!!!" Albert yelled.

Gabriel turned to Albert in surprise...

"What's not time? What the hell are you talking about Albert?"

The dusty whirl wind was a giant of a funnel. Albert charged towards it fighting the terror as he ran to get the kids. Gabriel followed. The rainbow aurora of light blinked out. The funnel dissipated, dropping to the ground instantly. Ten foot high tendrils of dust were all that remained. Before Albert could get to the fence, the lantern on the rear of the caboose lit up with a light so fiercely intense, it seemed to sear its way through the windows of the railcar.

Only a few moments before, the kids were standing on the rear landing as the giant spectacularly rainbow-coloured dusty funnel slowly, silently whirled around them. Daniel had stepped off the platform and headed out through the dense reeds. The others followed him off the platform.

"Neat!!!" they thought, as they wandered through the dust. A strange static with tiny sparks emanated off them. Their hair rose slightly. They were all giggling and laughing at each others' hair rising from the electrical static. Their silhouettes faded away as they walked through the dust from the caboose into the tall reeds. They had made their way out not more than a hundred feet through the reeds when an icy coldness fell over them. They all dropped below in the tall six foot high reeds. They huddled together. It was warm below, among the reeds. The cold air swept by above them. The sky was once again visible.

Dianne [Di-Di], Gordon, Benny, Georgi, Vera and Beverly lay out on the warm reeds. Devin, Daniel and Jacob crouched down not wanting to damage the three bows of Uncle Albert's. The funnel above them had vanished along with the strange aurora of light and sparking static. It had all been replaced by the quiet howl of a gentle warm wailing wind. It was cozy below the top of the high reeds. No wind. Just the suns warm rays beating down. No one had noticed that the reeds that they were sitting in had subtly changed their hue from a yellowish green to a greenish yellow. No one was calling for them.

Daniel was the first to stand up. He could feel and hear the wail of the warm wind about his face. His hair blew around from the back of his head. His shirt pressed against his back while it flapped on his arms and chest. His attention was on Uncle Albert's diary which he had taken out of his backpack to read. He had stuffed it in there while in the caboose. It was in good condition. He closed the diary and placed it back into his knapsack. He turned to go back to the caboose and then... looked up. He froze.

His lips parted as his jaw slowly dropped.

THE AWAKENING

Eduard never finished his call. The receiver hung by the chord some three feet below the phone box. A woman's voice was calling out from the receiver.

"Eduard ... Eduard ... are you still there??"

Eduard was staring out the little side door window facing the farm yard and the slough. The woman on the other end of the line was still calling his name.

Eduard had seen it ... again. He slowly stumbled backward with his eyes transfixed on the slowly fading funnel that engulphed the slough. He bolted for the back door with a crash as the door banged against the wall. He nearly knocked his mother over. Mable was very concerned that something ominous had just happened. Eduard's behaviour frightened her.

Eduard! Eduard!! TELL ME WHAT'S GOING ON!!!

Eduard threw himself off the porch ... "NOT NOW MOM!!!" and flew into his truck and roared backwards into the farm yard while doing a ninety degree turnaround in the dust.

Albert stood speechless in the reeds surrounding the caboose. His entire attention was riveted to that railcar.

Gabriel yelled ... "Albert!! What's going on?? Speak to me!!"

Albert and Gabriel made their way to the front platform. Albert noticed the dogs had probably run into the caboose. Deep down he knew ... he knew he was too late. He rushed the front platform of the caboose, sprinted up onto the landing and swung the door open. He was greeted with silence. Gabriel bounded up the railcar's platform behind Albert.

"Speak to me ... Albert!!"

Albert noticed the rear door was open. He entered the railcar.
Albert's heart sank. He was already calculating their probability of survival. He searched the interior quickly and was relieved that the kits were gone. They had taken the three bows and quiver of arrows with them. More importantly, they had tried on the knapsacks and were most likely wearing them when they stepped off the caboose. Even his First Aid manual and diary were gone. He hated the thought of losing the diary but, the kids needed it now just to survive. Even the tarpaulin and comforters were gone. At least that'll keep them warm nights.

His anger towards the missing diary turned into relief. They were probably playing as if they were on safari. Trust them to do the right thing at the wrong time. But this time, it was for real, and only he, Albert, knew what they were about to walk into. His upper teeth clamped down on his lower lip and he winced. He walked to the rear door and looked out. They and the three dogs were gone.

"They were in the hands of Providence Now" ... Albert thought.

He wished them a great journey, if they survived. He sighed deeply, thinking of his family. His family were going to skin him alive. Albert sank down upon the rear platform. His knees just then were way too weak to hold him up. He was slowly succumbing to shock.

Gabriel stood beside Albert and began calling for the kids. He scanned his eyes across the vast slough. He saw no movement. He kept calling. Finally he began to call Beverly by name. She would respond. Surely she would. Silence and stillness stared back.

"Where are they?" Gabriel thought to himself.

He leaned on the railing and turned slowly to Albert...

"Where are the kids? Albert!!

Where are the damn kids?"

Gabriel, for the first time, was beginning to panic.

"Albert!!"

Albert turned to Gabriel ... "There's something I have to tell you. It's about this slough. It's about this caboose."

Albert turned his gaze down to the bottom of the platform.

"You need to sit down."

Gabriel was silent as he stood there looking down at Albert's figure. Bewildered would be a more proper term to describe Gabriel's mental state.

"Look Albert. I just want to know where my little sister is, alright?"

Albert looked back up at Gabriel. "She's with them. They're all gone Gabe ... and there's no getting them back."

Gabriel sputtered "What do you mean they're gone? You're not making any sense Albert ... what the hell happened to the kids? Is this some kind of joke? Gabriel looked up and across the slough of reeds. "They're probably out there in the reeds hiding ... right?"

Albert was silent. Too silent. Too depressed.

"What the hell was going on here?" Gabriel thought. Gabriel looked down at Albert, and then slowly, sat down beside him. He wasn't overly worried. Just a little concerned about Albert's behaviour.

Albert quietly began ... "In 1943..."

. . .

Daniel was having difficulty adjusting to the new reality. He slowly turned his head left as far as he could, then to the right. He turned his body around to face the kids lying in the reeds below but, his eyes were still focussed on the horizon. Benny and Devin sat up, observing the surprise ... no ... fear would be a better description, of the peculiar expression that flowed over Daniel's face. Devin and Jacob turned slowly to look at each other. They both got up. Devin stood up in front of Daniel looking over Daniel's left shoulder. Jacob was scanning the horizon where Daniel was gawking. Something had changed.

"Where's the caboose?"

Devin then looked over Daniel's right shoulder to his father's place.

"Where's the farm?"

Daniel murmured ... "the question is, where are we?"

The strange conversation alerted everyone. The other six children stood up in unison. All eyes were searching the distant landscape. The landscape all around them was flat ... right to the horizon. It was all grassland interspersed here and there with little groves of trees. No caboose, no roads, no slough, no farms ... anywhere. Dorothy's family wasn't in Kansas anymore.

No one panicked quite yet. It was just all ... surreal. Then a sound that made them all turn instantly. It was whining or was it the wind? It was coming from where the caboose used to be.

"Devin! Jake!"... Daniel whispered.

He had taken the bow off and laid an arrow on it pulling back the string carefully, only an inch or two to maintain some tension just in case he had to draw it back quickly. Devin and Jacob did the same. They walked back the hundred or so feet. The rest followed closely. Devin, Daniel and Jacob opened up the distance between them. It was whining. Definitely not the wind. The sound stopped. The boys closed in until they were almost on top of the three dogs. Daniel looked up incredulously into Devin's face. Devin exchanged the same look and then lay down his spear placing the bow back on his shoulder. Daniel likewise strapped his bow back on his shoulder while putting his arrow back into the quiver.

There was Mickey, Towzer and Skipper. But they were all barely six weeks old.

"Skipper?" Devin called out as he picked the puppy up.

Benny looked at Daniel. "How...?"

Dianne picked up Towzer. Gordon picked up Mickey. Daniel was speechless. Gordon, becoming a little frightened, caught Daniel's eyes.

"Where are we Daniel?"

He gazed at Gordon, then looked up, not wanting to appear panicked but, couldn't reassure him.

"I ... don't ... know"

His voice trailing off as he slowly turned to scan the horizon once more. Gordon turned to look at the pup. He was the last to leave the railcar and turned to glance at the three mutts inside before stepping off with his siblings. He put it together in an instant, although, it made no real sense to any of them. Nothing made any sense now.

"The dogs must've been in the caboose" ... Gordon suggested.

Devin retorted..." What's that old railcar got to do with any of this?"

Gordon wasn't sure. He didn't know quite how to come to terms with everything that just happened. No one did.

Daniel was convinced...

"It was the marsh itself that conjured up that strange whirl wind with the strange aurora of lights above it. And what was with that weird static ... the sparks?"

They all looked at one another ... exchanging bewildered glances. Now what?

A summer breeze blew across the landscape. They were all standing. All quiet. Worried ... as the strangeness spread out before them to the distant horizon. So. What happens now?

Daniel perked up ... "Albert's diary! We've got Albert's diary! He's been here!"

Daniel removed the diary to read. They all gathered around and sat down in the deep shoulder height grass. He went to the last pages of the massive book. What he read sank his heart.

"The caboose has released me after twenty long years. I'm back. Nothing has changed. I'm the same age I was when I left. Had anyone known I had gone? It looked as though no time had ever passed. It was like taking a walk back in time and seeing everyone again. The brakeman and two conductors who disappeared before me never made it back. I met them in what I can only guess was somewhere in the Pleinsbachian. At least my geological time chart indicates the Pleinsbachian time or Stage was located somewhere deep in the early to middle Jurassic ..."

Daniel's head snapped up. "Jurassic? What's Uncle Albert talking about?" He closed the book, stood up again and took another look around.

"This ain't the Jurassic" he said to himself. "This is somewhere else." Yet ... it was eerily familiar somehow. He looked up at the sky. They had to find shelter and quickly. He targeted a grove of trees about a kilometre and a half away. It dawned on him how very vulnerable they all were out here ... where ever out here was. He, Jacob and Beverly were the oldest. They were responsible for this little troop of explorers.

Safety and shelter were the first consideration ... a fire second ... water third ... food last. This was the list of priorities. Crap. They better get moving. Later, they have to find out where the hell they are. The children carefully put the puppies in their respective knapsacks. It was time to move out.

He could tell by the trees and ground vegetation, they were in some sort of temperate climate not unlike where they once lived. This was still crazy but they had to adjust quickly because everything was beginning to look all too real. It seemed way too real to be a dream. Even if it was, he couldn't take the chance that it wasn't. Everyone's life hung in the balance.

The tall grass stretched out before them in all directions. If this was anything like Africa, the grasslands could hold potential dangers ... perhaps a large predator. What if there were a whole pride of predators? They could all be lost before they hit the safety of the grove ... providing there wasn't something waiting for them there as well. He didn't like the uncertainty. Too many ways to die out here.

The trees looked like they could be climbed, but they were a long way off. It was beginning to look frightening. They were all just too young to have any hope of surviving on their own. If they ran for the trees, their movement and noise might attract unwelcome curiosity ... sighting and then targeting them as a potential meal.

They had to be cautious ... very cautious and deliberate in their every move.

Daniel sat everyone down. He explained their situation,
trying not to alarm everyone. They had to stick tightly together, close to himself, Devin and Jacob ... but behind them. Devin, Daniel and Jacob possessed weapons that could do serious damage or even kill. Their first near death experience was almost upon them as Daniel decided to try out one of the bows. He didn't want to lose the arrow and at nine years of age he made his first and nearly fatal error in judgement.

Without much thought he turned to the group and explained that he was going to see just what the range of their weapons really were. He found the bow to have a pretty taught string. He aimed skyward, straight up and drew back the string. Devin and Jacob immediately followed Daniel's movement. All three arrows were loosed as the three bows each made a loud "thoop". They were amazed. The three arrows climbed out of sight.

Little five year-old Gordon was the first ... "Where'd they go?"

All were looking upwards shielding their eyes from the glare of the sun. Daniel began to speak ...

"Don't worry ... whatever goes up is gonna" ... the next word out of his mouth as his brain connected the dots was one of sheer terror ...

"RUUUUUUN!!!"

Everybody connected the dots instantly. They scrambled in every direction ... except Gordon. The first arrow penetrated the ground at least a foot deep barely three feet from him. Gordon jumped as he snapped his head towards the arrow while executing a one hundred eighty degree turn backwards in full sprint mode. The second arrow punched into the ground barely four feet in front of him. The third arrow stabbed into Georgi's backpack as he let out a yelp.

. . .

As Eduard hurtled down the old dusty road in his pick-up leading away from the farm, a dust cloud rose behind him. Albert and Gabriel hadn't noticed ... or didn't care. Gabriel was too concerned about what Albert was telling him. Albert was concerned about the children's ultimate fate. If only he hadn't left that damned caboose to put that flask of whisky back. But then again, how did that bolt of lightening become the triggering mechanism behind this new "event"??

Within five minutes, Eduard was standing on the road across from his pick-up, facing the caboose. He was hesitant. No one was in sight. He felt that fear slam into his chest once again. This time, he was within ten meters of the terror. He called out. No answer. He called out again. Only silence called back. Now he was angry as well as terrified. He screamed at the top of his lungs...

"ALBERT!!! UNCLE ALBERT!!! GABE!!!

Eduard was shaking like a leaf.

"The old slough had taken them all" ... he thought.

"What the Jesus hell was going on???"

Gabriel sat beside Albert in total disbelief attempting to figure out whether or not Albert was insane or whether he had just revealed the greatest secret known to Man ... here ... on this farm ... in this railcar. He couldn't swallow this story. It was just too preposterous.

"Yet ... where were the kids?" Gabriel thought.

He quietly got up and stepped down the railing of the caboose onto the ground and stood chest deep in the five foot tall reeds. They had to be hiding, Gabriel thought. He bent over and checked the underside of the railcar. Nobody was there. He slowly stood back up. He was having a difficult time accepting Albert's story at face value. He was oblivious to everything else around him as he struggled to make sense of the situation.

Eduard tucked in his fear and began making his way through the reeds of marsh grass towards the caboose. He approached the front platform and swung up onto the first step. He hesitated. He slowly clambered up the next few steps. He was now facing the door.

The dogs were gone. He called out their names one by one. Gabriel could hear Eduard. Perhaps one of the kids would respond. The kids knew Eduard. They knew how far they could push his patience. Eduard's voice was attaining a pitch of anger. Gabriel knew that now was the time for the kids to respond ... surely. Silence answered back.

"No way they wouldn't have answered him unless ... they were gone." Eduard thought to himself.

He shuddered at the thought. He opened the door and looked in. Once again Eduard hesitated to step in. That creepy fear was crawling up his spine again. There was nothing in the caboose. It was as if nothing had ever been there. He walked in. He headed towards the rear door, unlatched it and quietly pushed it open. He turned slowly to look back behind him ... as if something in the small confines of the caboose was closing in on him. It was spine tingling terror.

Albert, who had been quietly sitting on the rear platform turned to Eduard and called out his name. The sound of his name being called out of nowhere took Eduard completely by surprise. Eduard's heart skipped a beat as he fell out the door against the rear landing rail sprinting backwards all the while executing a sloppy, uncoordinated, backward somersault, legs and arms splayed out as he launched himself in a mid-air flight down the other side of the rear landing steps screaming a single obscenity ...

"SHIIIIIIIIIIIIIITTT!!!!"

Then silence as his body crumpled into the tall grass, his legs splayed open as they lay upward on the rear steps of the caboose.

Albert turned quietly ... "Are you all right ... Ed ... Eduard?"

Eduard lay upside down with his legs splayed on the rear landing steps on the other side of the railcar, all the while clutching his heart, breathing deeply ... rapidly.

"Don't EVER...EVER!!!"

Eduard caught himself.

Albert quietly uttered ... "Sorry."

Eduard detected a quiet loss in Albert's voice. Eduard brought himself back to the memory of that strange and beautiful whirl wind funnel.

He got up painfully. "Did you see it Albert??"

"Yes" ... Albert said softly...

"I saw it Eduard. I saw it ... all too well."

Eduard stepped back up on the platform, hands on his hips, his back arched rearwards, grunting with pain, looking down at Albert's folded form. He saw Gabriel at the bottom, in the reeds, gazing out at the slough. Eduard glanced down at Albert...

"Where are the kids? ...Uncle?"

Albert turned and looked up at Eduard...

"They're gone."

Eduard was speechless. Albert got up and motioned Eduard back into the caboose. Gabriel turned and followed them back in. Eduard's eyes followed his uncle into the caboose. Albert sat down heavily. Eduard and Gabriel both entered the caboose and sat down with him ... ears open and giving Albert, for once, their complete and undivided attention.

ACCUSATIONS

No matter what happened now, Eduard thought, there was a lot of explaining to do. Eduard's mother was going to be uncontrollably livid. The entire family were going to absolutely go off the deep end. For the time being, Eduard knew his life had turned into one very big, disconcerting pile of dung ... He felt sick to his stomach. None of the three moved or said a word for a full minute.

Turning to his uncle, Eduard, in an accusatory tone, looked directly into Albert's face

... "I thought you said we were safe for at least another eight years!!"

Albert turned to him, shaking, with his voice quivering ... "I don't know what the hell's going on anymore ... I just don't" ... his voice trailed off.

Eduard continued ... "Albert ... you think that bolt of lightning had anything to do with it?"

Albert turned to Eduard ... "That did have a lot of power ... didn't it? Maybe that's a clue?"

Gabriel interjected, "What the hell are you guys talking about? One or both of you had better start making some sense here."

Eduard sighed and sat back against the bench.

"...A clue to what Albert? Fifty years in a loony bin?"

Eduard put his hands together between his knees, bowing his head as if to pray.

"I believe you uncle. I really do but, Albert, do you have any idea how deep in the crapper we are?"

Eduard sat up...

"This is the second disappearance involving you ... Uncle. The authorities are really going to try to hang you on this one ... and now Gabriel and I are accomplices ... damn it ..."

Albert was sitting straight up, eyes glued to one of the dirty windows...

"Three!"

Eduard turned to his uncle. "Three? What are you talking about Uncle?"

Albert turned slowly to Eduard with a slightly cocked head, a stern look and raised eyebrows. Eduard's memory was jolted.

"Oh ... yes ... that ..."

Albert looked across at Gabriel.

"Tell him Eduard ... what you told me."

Eduard got up, went into his pocket and pulled out a second flask. He poured himself, Gabriel and Albert two stiff drinks. No coffee. He banged the flask on the table. He handed Albert and Gabriel their drinks. Eduard swallowed his down in one gulp. He poured another for himself. Albert followed. He took the flask from Eduard and poured himself a second drink as well. All three sat there silently, each holding a glass of whiskey, sipping occasionally, each trying to think out logically not what happened but, how in the Jesus hell any of them were going to explain this to their family and the rest of the outside world.

Albert, looking down, quietly muttered...

"I'm going to shoot myself ... yes ... that'll save me."

Eduard nodded.

"You know what's funny uncle? I ran out of shotgun shells yesterday."

A few moments later, Albert lapsed into a kind of depression...

"We lost the kids ... we can't shoot ourselves because you ran out of shotgun shells ... what next?"

Unknown to the three men, a second storm had arrived. The wind had increased and the caboose was beginning to sway. Rain began to pelt down onto the railcar. The rain was drumming loudly now. All three stared out the dirty windows. Albert finished off his drink and looked down at the floor.

"Now it's raining on our caboose."

Fifteen silent seconds had passed as the rain pelted their caboose, before Eduard and Albert turned to each other and burst out laughing. Eduard couldn't stop. Albert fell over onto the bench ... fist pounding into the old wooden seat, barely able to speak

"...and ... and ... do you know what?"... Eduard giggled,

"I nearly took the door off its hinges coming out the rear of the caboose ..."

"I just about swallowed my tobacco when you flew off the rear steps" Albert blurted out.

Eduard was on the floor. Albert rolled off the bench. The laughter continued unabated then ... suddenly ... stopped. Both men were breathing heavily. The stress had been completely released. Gabriel sat there chuckling to himself. Now a silent dread had taken hold as the two men lay together on the floor. Gabriel could only think of his little sister ... Beverly.

Eduard turned to his Uncle...

"What are we going to do Albert?"

Albert sat up on the floor with a great sigh...

"I can't face them again Eduard."

"That makes two of us Albert. If only another lightning bolt would take the three of us from here."

Eduard could scarcely believe he actually said that out loud but, this time he truly meant it.

"That works for me..." Albert shot back.

Gabriel turned his head slightly. With heavy sighs and grunting, both men got up off the floor. Eduard was the first to speak.

"...Time to face the music"

Albert sighed...

"I'm glad I'm not facing it alone Eduard."

All of a sudden Eduard had a premonition.

"What if people decided to burn this caboose to the ground? Would that seal the fate of the kids?"

Albert himself was now worried about the possibility.

"We have to protect this caboose ... at all costs Eduard."

Gabriel interjected...

"No one's going to burn down just this caboose guys. They're going to lock us all inside THEN burn it down."

Gabriel continued...

"So this thing has been in the family for some time now ? Why didn't anybody same something ?" Gabriel thought for a moment, weighing what he just said.

"Okay. Forget I asked that."

He was thinking to himself. It was true. The kids were in fact gone. So were the dogs. We would have heard them by now. The equipment was also. That would have slowed them down considerably. Gabriel turned to Albert.

"Let's hear the whole story Albert ... from the beginning ... again".

The story of twenty years was compressed into an hour and a half. Both Eduard and Gabriel were bombarding him with questions to search for any inconsistencies in Albert's story. There were none. Gabriel got up and headed for the door. He needed to take this all in. That dust devil was one of the weirdest things he had ever seen in his life. It was then that the truth finally sank in for Gabriel. He turned to see both men stand and walk towards the front door.

This was heading out to be a long day for all three. The men then, walked out of the caboose, into the reeds and up onto the gravelled road turning one last time for a long glance at the strange caboose then, climbed into their respective cars. They drove to Willie J's.

That night, Mable was finally having it out with Albert. Willie J. interceded several times to calm his wife down. She lit into Eduard for taking Albert's side. Mable stormed upstairs and slammed the door. The men stood silent. Mable was crying. Willie left his son, brother and Gabriel in the living room to attend to Mable. The yelling upstairs began again. Eduard glanced at Albert and Gabriel...

"This is just the beginning. Someone has to relate all of this to Evelyn and Rolf, Deanna and Steven, Bill and Dorothy as well as Manfred and Gardenia."

Eduard felt it was his responsibility even though none were truly responsible for the disappearance of those kids. Eduard glanced out the living room window

"...God, what a mess."

A flash of lightning lit up the living room, startling everyone. The rain lasted all night long.

Eduard and Gabriel decided to go to Albert's place to sleep. Eduard wanted to make sure Albert wasn't alone. A cup of hot tea at Albert's might settle them in for the night. They left without word. The crash upstairs told them that Mable was throwing things and in a very nasty mood, but who wouldn't be?

After breakfast and coffee, the next morning, Eduard, Gabriel and Albert went out the door down the steps of Albert's home, only to be greeted by the RCMP with their hands on their revolvers.

"Step away from the door!! ..." one Mountie shouted.

There were some six police cruisers with their blue and red lights beaming out around Albert's yard accompanied by a dozen officers. They had just arrived. All three men were handcuffed with their hands behind their back. The Press was there, shooting a gallery of photos.

"Great ... now our photos were going to be splashed all over Canada, possibly the States as potential mass murderers." Eduard thought to himself.

Albert sighed deeply. Gabriel closed his eyes and rolled his head back. He couldn't believe how one little picnic was inching them towards international infamy. One officer told them that they were being taken in for questioning. All three men got their attorneys. They were being held at the RCMP detachment in Morden.

The town was abuzz with excitement. It was quickly becoming the news event of the nation. Both attorneys for their respective clients ordered the men released if no charges were being laid. For now, Albert, Eduard and Gabriel were free but under severe court restrictions. A throng of journalists besieged the court offices in Morden. Eduard decided that they should both go to Albert's and wait out the day there even though Albert's place was surrounded by journalists.

Their attorneys accompanied them and warned the Press about harassment charges. The men had not been charged with any crime. After being released on their own cognisance, Eduard, Gabriel and Albert decided to go to Willie Js. and Mable's. There, they met a quieter atmosphere. The family had the same attorney. It was costing a fortune. Mable was convinced that Albert was responsible for all their current misfortune.

Their attorney warned the Press that they would be charged for trespassing if they set foot anywhere on the Morley land. For now, even the authorities were warning the Press about interfering with a criminal investigation. They had roped off the area around the caboose. The Press were camped out on the gravelled road. It was a circus.

"How did it ever come to this?" ... sighed Eduard.

With Evelyn's hysteria, Gardenia and Manfred's anger and the other visiting aunts and uncles, there was no more "home sweet home". That was in the past now. Everything was coming apart.
No one believed Eduard, Gabriel or Albert. How could they? Yet, within their respective families, no one truly believed that they could have been responsible. Even Mable was coming around. After all, she knew her son all too well. If he was sticking up for Albert, at the cost of his own reputation with family and friends, perhaps, she was wrong about Albert as well.

The RCMP investigation was ongoing.

Eight months later, only a couple of junior reporters were camped out near the farm of Willie Js. Finally even they were called in.

The Morley clan were no longer centre stage newsworthy. Other events overshadowed them. The RCMP also toned down their investigation but never for a moment closed it off. No more clues came in. The entire investigation stalled for want of any more leads. It was now on their backburner but never forgotten. A year had passed.

Evelyn and Thomas were forced to start a new life. Manfred and Gardenia fared no better. The stress was too great for Gardenia who later died of a pulmonary arrhythmia. Manfred spiralled into a deep depression. He gave up the farm two years later. He moved to Larvyer. Eight years later, Willie J. and Mable moved to Pilot Mound to reboot their lives. Mable was convinced that God had taken her grandchildren safely to Heaven. But it rang hollow. For the very first time in her life, her faith was badly shaken.

Rolf's booming floor covering business on Winnipeg's Kennedy Street continued and partially helped to take his mind off his family's loss. Eduard moved to Portage La Prairie after his parents moved to the "Mound" and met a young lady ... Anastasia. They got married and had two little one's of their own ... Suzanne and Samuel.

Steve and Deanna moved to Regina. Dorothy wanted to stay in Nesbitt close to Larvyer and Morley Lake but, Bill convinced her to move back with him to Edmonton where they eventually retired.

Gabriel decided to move to Nesbitt the following year after the disappearance of his sister and went into seclusion. Occasionally, he quietly made the trip to the Morley farm unannounced and wandered around in the reeds of the slough.

Albert busied himself with his clockwork passion. It was a good distraction from the event that changed all their lives so utterly. On some nights, Albert would drop everything and walk out in the country under the stars and contemplate on all that had transpired in their lives. It was going to be another very cold, isolating winter.

The farms had been purchased by a farming conglomerate. They reserved the land for a later future project and let the farms go to seed. It was the land only that they were interested in.

As time passed the buildings on both farms fell into ruin. Some collapsed. The farm houses themselves had no furniture. They were barren and slowly collapsed. The wooden frame of Willie Js and Mable's house that they worked so hard to keep up had begun to warp, breaking the windows and allowing Nature to slip inside. The inside porch door to the kitchen was hanging by a single latch. The outside porch door was lying on the ground. The screen door was banging in the wind as each storm appeared and went. The entire farm was undergoing a transition as much as the farm folk that once lived there.

The farm machinery lay about like rusted out fossil hulks. They were quickly disintegrating. The ghosts of past Christmases, holiday dinner celebrations, picnics in the fields and other memories whispered in the sirens of sound accompanied by the winds as they blew incessantly over the long strands of forgotten telephone wires that had not yet broken off the poles that they were still attached to. The once powerful yard light under which the family played football now lay undignified on the ground. Two of the grey barns had collapsed crushing the old buggy and model T stowed under their roofs.

Nature's reclamation project was actually a very pretty sight. Weeds had overgrown everything. Wild flowers were everywhere dotting the landscape like splashes from an artists brush. The farm funeral, as buildings were slowly lowered onto the ground by Nature was given one last salute as Nature threw its flowers all over the macabre scene.

One was witnessing a real funeral unfolding in slow motion and it was a very pretty spectacle to behold. Only Nature could do it with such grace.

The small hamlet of Nesbitt was reduced from twelve homes to just three. The town of Carroll fared no better. The grain elevators and train stations all vanished. The CPR rails were gone, torn up. Carroll now had only five or six homes and the old massive stone school where all the McIntyres' had been educated had been converted into a single family home.

The farms of William James Morley and his oldest son Manfred Morley were now effectively gone and buried. A few fence posts stood quietly as grave markers to what were once two lively farms with one hundred years of memories ... never to rise again.

The other farms of the Morley clan continued. No one from these clans ever ventured onto these "death lands". No one ever fished or hunted there again. Morley Lake was nicknamed Morbid Lake or Death Lake by the town folk.

Every year and a half, someone, somewhere, passing that forbidding and lonely landscape would report seeing a giant swirling twister engulf the entire marsh. Sometimes the strange whirl wind appeared in summer as whirling fog or even dust topped by a magnificent multihued aurora (so they said). In the middle of winter it appeared like a swirling snow storm.

It was also said that the ominous snow white clad figure of "Jack Frost" would make an appearance to watch it. This lonely figure, it was said, quietly stalked the marshlands at those times. The towns folk said the ghostly figure had an eerie resemblance to an old man they once knew that lived in the area ... Albert Morley.

It still drew curious onlookers and the stories became enhanced.

Alien abduction and opening of inter-dimensional gateways were all the rage as were stories of a Canadian version of Jack the Ripper still on the loose around these prairie towns. The townsfolk from all around that site called this stealthy killer of small children "Jack Frost". It made Christmases a little scarier around Larvyer. But it was damn good for business. For a while, Larvyer boomed as a macabre tourist attraction.

ALICE IN WONDERLAND

After the arrows had returned to Earth, the boys walked over to pick them up and place them back in their quivers. Daniel's heart was still pounding. The three boys had better find a lot more respect for their weapons if they were to avoid killing each other.

Devin looked at Jacob and Daniel...

"We don't do that again..."

Daniel and Jacob nodded back in agreement. For now, the little troop of children had gathered together once more for the trek to the nearest grove of trees. The only dangerous creatures they encountered so far were each other. That was scary enough.

Daniel, Devin and Jacob took the lead. Bennie and Gordon followed closely behind Devin as they began their trek through the five foot tall grass. It was these two that carried an eight foot long spear each. Fully one quarter was a triangular metal arrowhead of crafted steel. Beverly carried the third spear. Everyone was taking care not to make any noise as they blindly made their way through the grasslands. Benny, Devin and Georgi watched the troop's rear. Five year old Di-Di simply stayed close to Daniel where he genuinely wanted her. He might have to pick her up quickly if pressed to.

As instructed by Daniel, everyone kept quiet as they made their way through the grasslands. Daniel knew they had no chance against a ravenous pack of hunter killers. If they made it to the grove and up one of the massive oaks, they could easily survive for another day. They could deal with one predator at a time. They may be juveniles but, they were primate juveniles with big and complex brains. They could figure things out. In time, experience would aid in their survival.

They had to stay very tightly knit together so that Di-Di, Vera, and Gordon could see Devin, Daniel, Beverly and Jacob's hand signals above the grass. For now, two hand signals would do ... palm flat and up meant "freeze". A nodding closed fist forward finger point meant "continue". In the backpacks were eleven floppy leather hats of which the children put on nine of them, to protect them from sunburn and the scorching heat in the middle of god knows where.

And so ... the journey commenced.

The sun continued to beat down on the little rag-tag band of nine child explorers. Daniel wished almost for a thunderstorm, to conceal their presence out here in the vastness of nowhere. It was about five thousand feet; nearly a full mile to the first grove of trees....About five trees in all. And they were big, even from this distance. They had gotten around fifteen hundred feet from their original starting point when something very peculiar made its presence known to the small band of child explorers.

Everyone stopped. They listened.

"What is that?" Benny inquired. The children looked around. The horizon was clear.

Daniel motioned for them to continue. This they did for another sixty or so feet. The sound continued unabated. It was distant thunder. Daniel was somewhat relieved. Maybe a storm was forming after all. It was Bennie who was the first to notice. On the horizon far, far behind them, low forming clouds were accumulating.

"I knew it!!" ... thought Daniel.

It was a fast approaching storm. They quickened their pace. They had gone another five hundred feet or so when Benny again turned around to look back. He stopped and loudly called out to Daniel. Daniel, Devin and Jacob whipped around. "

"What was Benny doing yelling out like that??"

"Gawd damn it!!" Daniel murmured ..."Didn't I instruct him as to the dangers out here!?!"

It then hit Daniel that something was terribly wrong. The colour of the cloud was a yellowish brown ... not blue, white, gray or purple. That, and the now strange fact that the rumbling was constant. Benny snapped his head around once again to glance at the older boys. Daniel, Jacob, Devin, Georgi and Beverly were all frozen, with their gaze transfixed and locked onto the approaching storm. Then slowly, they turned to each other.

Devin whispered loudly...

"It sounds like a heard of cattle... just like in those cowboy shows."

"No ... wait ... a stampede???" Jacob said quietly.

"A stampede of what?" Daniel asked himself.

It was bigger, much bigger than a herd of cattle he thought. Daniel turned and glanced at the grove of trees some three thousand feet away. His heart was pounding. They weren't going to make it. Too far, way too far. Benny and Devin could already make out tiny moving brown dots in the yellowish-brown cloud which stretched across nearly a quarter of their existing horizon. Jacob and Daniel quickly exchanged glances. Panic was beginning to set in. The little crew started to back up.

Daniel yelled...

"Everyone!! ... Start running for the grove!!" He knew, deep down, that their little safari group just wasn't going to make it. They were dead. There was no way out. He had to think ... and fast. He scoured the landscape ahead of him as he ran. In one spot not more than six or seven hundred feet away, directly in front of them, on their way to the grove was what appeared to be a thicket of branches, sticking up some seven, maybe eight feet above the grass and about fifty or sixty feet veering just left of where they were headed. Could it be a fallen tree? He shouted loudly to everyone while pointing in rapid, jerking arm movements

"Run for your lives towards that thicket of branches."

He picked up Dianne and instructed Georgi to grab Gordon. Jacob was Daniel's height and the strongest of all of them. He grabbed Vera. They were now running awkwardly through the thickets of tall grass for everything they were worth, heading to what they hoped was salvation. It was still too far. The ground was starting to shake. The sound of rumbling was quite loud. They were still some two hundred feet away when the crash of thundering hooves was nearly upon them. No one dared look back.

Within fifty feet of their destination, they could hear the beasts calling out to one another. That was way too close. They weren't going to make it Daniel thought. He was almost out of breath when the first big animal passed him.

They were bison ... tens of thousands of them.

Daniel tucked both he and Di-Di's heads down and crashed through the upright branches. Gordon struggled to get up on the oak trunk. Gordon, crying, screamed

"I can't get..."

Devin, unceremoniously ... yanked him over with Georgi pushing him from behind. Benny crawled up and over the tree trunk bruising his knees. The older boys yanked Beverly and Vera over. Then Jacob sprinted in last, making sure no one got left behind. A two thousand pound bison caught up to him and from behind, it brushed him aside sending him directly in the path of another bison that turned to adjust only slightly its forward path before slamming the side of its body into Jacob and catapulting Daniel's cousin over the oak trunk. Daniel was thankful they all made it. He could no longer be heard as the giant silhouettes in the dust thundered around them. He motioned everyone to take cover behind the dead tree trunk.

At that very instant, a bison breached the branches straight over the dead tree trunk crashing down in their midst. Daniel tried hard not to pee himself but to no avail. Adrenaline was cascading through him like a waterfall. Everyone was under the tree trunk as the massive herd crashed over the top of them like a thundering waterfall. It was truly terrifying.

The terror mounted as one of the bison lost its footing while trying to clear the tree trunk. It fell. Then another one tripped over the bison on the ground. Soon, three bison were down. Two managed to get back up. One was having difficulty. It was still on the ground, on its side kicking wildly barely three feet from where they lay. The hooves thrust out, kicking into the oak just inches from where Devin and Gordon lay ... sending up a shower of tree bark. The two children were screaming. They had no where to go. The animal eventually got its footing again and was up and gone, pursuing the herd.

It was only five minutes but it seemed an eternity before the thundering waterfall of hooves started to dissipate. A few stragglers passed on either side. It was over. The children were safe. They were choking in the dust which was rapidly clearing.

"Devin!! Jake!!" Daniel called out.

He quickly fixed an arrow upon his bow. Devin and Jacob witnessing this followed his move. They realised Daniel's concern. What got such a massive herd on the run like that? It had to be some sort of predators. All three boys scanned the horizon. There was nothing in sight.

"Quickly!!" Daniel yelled out.

Everybody checked out okay. No serious or life threatening injuries save Benny's skinned knees and Vera with her sore arm from being jerked over the dead tree trunk. Jacob's sides were slightly sore after his brush with the two bison.

And the race was on again for the grove of trees. The grove was only about twenty two hundred feet away, but, a lot could still happen, between here and there. They weren't out of the woods yet.

Devin yelled in a loud whisper. "The herd seems to be turning!

"Hopefully not around again!" Georgi added with some trepidation.

Still ... maybe they had run into another batch of predators.
The pounding hooves were nearly a half mile off. The kids were still running. They were now some thirteen hundred feet away when Devin stopped dead ... to rest ... to catch his breath. Daniel was annoyed, but he too was exhausted. The rest drank from the three available canteens.

"Save the water ..." Devin scolded.

Daniel knew that if they sat down now, they might never get up for a while. He spurned them on at a more leisurely pace ... so long as they continued to shorten the dangerous distance between them and safety. Twenty five minutes had passed since that traumatic stampede of massive bison. The puppies were shaken up, but still safely tucked away in the knapsacks.

With enormous relief ... they had finally reached the grove. As they walked toward the trunk of the great oak, its long branches provided them with the dark shade of cool relief from the scorching sun. They quickened their pace as they approached the trunk. They all came to a halt when they reached the trunk to catch their breath.

Gordon slowly walked backward into Daniel and Jacob ... frightened by something he could not comprehend. They all turned. They were alerted to the rustling and the movement of the tips of the grass very close to them. They could see that there were three paths in the tall grass that were being parted open. Two were together, side by side. Another was some twenty feet off to their right. The movement through the grass was zeroing in on their position ... and fast.

Daniel's only thought ... "Oh shit!! Here we go again!! Get the little ones up into the tree!!"

Devin was pushing Gordon up the oak to the lowest branch twelve feet above them, while Daniel was tossing Di-Di up the trunk. The small branches extending from the bottom half of the trunk of the oak tree aided them greatly in climbing to that first massive branch. Jacob was already up and grabbing everyone onto that lower giant branch.

"Quick! Quick! Quick!" was the refrain from the two bow carriers at the base of the Oak.

Benny was next. He was up twice as fast. He turned to reach down and pull little Di-Di up with him. Beverly, the oldest and strongest of the girls pushed her up and then hurled Vera up behind her. Beverly quickly scaled the side of the oak and when she reached that first massive branch, kept pushing them up ever higher. The low reverberating guttural snarls were loud.

The terrors had arrived.

Devin and Daniel rapidly fixed an arrow on their respective bows. Without hesitation, Devin loosed the first arrow. It whizzed by one of the monstrous cave lions. They were twice as big as African lions. Daniel dropped his arrow on the ground cursing. Devin had turned and was already halfway up the trunk to the first branch.

Daniel started yelling at the lions ... motivated highly by fear. Devin reached the lower overhanging branch twelve feet off the ground as Benny, Beverly and Vera pulled him up. The others had simply climbed higher. Devin yelled at Benny and Jacob to pull Daniel up. Daniel was too frightened to turn his back on these enormous cats. Daniel from his perch only twelve feet off the ground let another arrow go.

Unsure of what they were facing, the tawny lions walked slowly forward. The lead cat screamed as it whipped around with an arrow embedded in its left shoulder. The other two lions snapped their heads towards the injured cat as they instinctively crouched, snarling their surprise.

Daniel was climbing for everything he was worth. He was extremely vulnerable. A second arrow buried itself in the ground in front of one of the cats, nicking its front toe, causing it to jump.

Benny grabbed the shaft of Daniel's spear as Daniel held it high in his fist. Both Benny and Devin together yanked Daniel up the twelve feet to the overhanging branch. All the while, Daniel was imagining one of the lions burying its talons in his ass and hurtling him off the tree. He was shaking like a leaf. He could hardly pull the next arrow out of the quiver. He felt like such a stupid klutz not realising that it was due to the effects of shock. He had difficulty steadying the arrow on his bow.

Devin noticed. "Give it to Benny!!"

He did so without question. Daniel was utterly useless. He could hardly balance himself on the branch, he was shaking so violently. He needed to climb higher but, would stay low enough to assist any of the others up to a higher perch.

The attack came swiftly.

Like a locomotive hurtling down the tracks, the first monster of a cat came charging through the grass, in to the trunk of the oak from below and launched itself straight up to a height of fifteen feet. The big cat with its piercing eyes glared straight up at Daniel, who in turn was reduced to a blubbering idiot out of sheer naked terror screaming at both Devin and Benny...

"SHOOT IT!!! SHOOT IT!!!
FOR CHRIST'S SAKE SHOOT IT!!!"

The big cat made a fatal move. It hesitated for only a second and turned its head sharply, glaring at Devin and Benny who, stomachs nearly dropping into their pants, simultaneously fired their volley at point blank range. Devin's arrow penetrated the great cat's huge muscular neck severing its spinal cord. Benny's arrow pierced the cat's eye, slicing through its brain.

The lioness dropped soundlessly ... its sharp talons scraping off a shower of bark as it fell ... its seven hundred pound body hitting the ground with a heavy thud. The second monster cat had already launched itself ... passing the other falling cat on its way up the trunk of the oak. It was enough to abort. It clung to the tree for a brief second or two then, leapt off the oak hitting the ground with an oomph, and scrambled back into the grasses.

The children were exhausted and quite traumatized. From their vantage point now, cringing in the tree tops, they could see the grasslands for miles. Still, they had to be extremely vigilante at night. The oak was an easy tree to climb. If they could do it ... so could the big cats.

In another culture, Benny and Devin would be receiving their first well earned eagle feathers.

The children climbed as high as they could. It was still daylight in their new world and Daniel wanted to read as much as he could of Albert's survival manual. The children gathered around, some fifty feet up the wide spreading oak to listen to Daniel's reading. Devin was instructed to see what they had in the way of food. The inventory was inadequate for any long term survival.

Albert's manual was well done with excellent hand drawn illustrations. Detail was everything to Albert. His survival manual was broken into geological Stages of earth history. In each Stage, lasting five to six million years, which Albert numbered one to one hundred twenty, he wrote down five categories;

A/ Food
B/ Shelter
C/ Weapons
D/ First Aid
E/ Fire and Cooking

Albert thought of everything. On the first page, he instructed any new explorers to start a tiny diary [included in one of the knapsacks with pencils and pencil-sharpener to keep track of each passing day and the transitioning cycles which would give them an idea of what Stage they were in]. This manual was meant for Albert alone, in case he desired a return to these strange worlds. This was so important ... Albert advised, in order to identify plants in each eco-system for food. It seemed from Albert's calculations that he had been trapped in each stage for as long as ninety one days or three months, give or take a few hours.

Daniel looked up at his small crew...

"I guess we're not going home anytime soon guys" ... he sighed.

Jacob sided up to Daniel and quietly whispered so as not to frighten the little ones...

"Dan...that's twenty years! Twenty years!" He breathed incredulously.

For now, the tiny crew would sleep the night out among the stars like any group of primates that lived in the trees. Daniel sat up reading until the light faded. He and Devin took turns watching the branches below them. Jacob and Beverly were worried about the dogs making any noise. They could accidentally alert the giant cats far below. Jacob found some string in one of the knapsacks. They would take some gauze from the First Aid kit, wrap it around the snout of any puppy who got noisy and secure it with string. It was the only way. The puppies had to be fed first ... just to keep them quiet. Georgi loved the dogs but was apprehensive about having them here. They could become a liability and endanger the lives of everybody concerned. Beverly interjected by suggesting that the little ones take care of the puppies.

"It would give them something to do ... something to care for ... to take their little minds off their situation."

A blanket was removed from a knapsack and used to cover Gordon, Di-Di and Vera. Daniel wound a rope around them lightly in case any of them slipped off the branch. Neither Devin, Daniel nor Jacob were any good at staying awake. Soon ... all were fast to sleep. They had completely let their guard down. They were woken in the middle of the night by the loud cacophony of giant cats in some sort of fight with growls and snarls emanating far below them. Di-Di started to cry. She was reassured by the others that the giants weren't coming up the tree. Daniel wasn't so sure about that. Neither were Devin or Jacob. The whole group were on a razor's edge, heightened by the loud and ever threatening terrors from below. After about an hour, the noise had abated. No one could see where the monsters were ... or what was happening below them. They knew the giant cats were still there... but where? What were they up to?

They were somewhere in the grasslands quite close to the oak and by the sounds they were making ... they realised that there were a lot more of them. They had no idea just how large in numbers, the pride of giant cats were. It was too terrifying to contemplate. They were trapped. It would be a long sleepless night for all of them.

Morning sunlight came early. As they slowly shuffled awake in the early morning cold, they were becoming ever more aware that this was not a dream.

Everyone continued to sleep for another hour and a half. Hunger got them stirring again. Daniel and Devin were still wearing the bows on their backs. Benny crawled over to Devin and then pointed downward putting his forefinger on his lips. He then went to Daniel as Devin looked down, gasped and froze. He turned to look up at his older cousin, waiting for a response. Daniel and Jacob went to get up when Benny put his finger on Daniel's lips and
Georgi alerted Jacob, quietly pointing down at the nine behemoth lions stretched out on the massive lower branches and in the grass all around the oak.

The mammoth sized cats had already eaten their dead comrade. One of the nine lions rested at the bottom of the great oak. It didn't have the strength to climb. It was panting in distress. It had an arrow lodged in its shoulder. Only a stub of the arrow shaft was now visible. It had bitten the protruding staff of the arrow clean off.

Everyone was now alerted to the extreme danger below their roost. There was no longer any doubt the children had picked the one oak among the one grove of trees that this lion pride called its home base or den. It was from this open air den that the pride surveyed its grassland domain. They had already eaten and could remain on the oak for days. Even if they left, a pride that huge must own a lot of territory far and wide from the epicentre of their giant oak den. The children had inadvertently walked themselves from the frying pan into the fire. If they used their weapons to remove the pride from the massive oak branches, the big cats would simply scatter into the grasses around the oak and wait for them to come down.

The dead lion was a result of a point blank shot. They may not be so lucky again. The child safari was in a fix. The only other alternative was to wait until the pride were on the hunt again and time their return or leave the oak altogether. That too was fraught with danger.

The next nearest grove, Daniel estimated, was some five hundred to seven hundred feet away ... and it was big. He could count as many as fifty or more trees. There also seemed to be a small waterway cutting through the grasslands. It was hard to make out as it was shielded by so many trees along its banks. It would afford a lot more protection and perhaps even drinking water. It was a dangerous gamble.

For now, they would have to bide their time on the last of their beef jerky. Relieving themselves up in the tree was another danger. Their scent could become a direct challenge to the pride. Yet, the pride of cats must know that they are up there. For now, it was a waiting game.

Daniel was content to read Albert's manual. Devin and Bennie watched the grasslands for any sign of potential game animals that might motivate the pride to leave their haunt. Gordon, Di-Di and Vera had the ropes tied around their waists and the top branches. To fall now was certain death. Benny, Devin, Jacob, Georgi and Beverly and Daniel did the same.

The puppies were placed into the tops of the knapsacks and a small piece of string wrapped in gauze was gently tied around their necks giving them a twelve inch leash lest they fall from the tree. It was risky doing it that way. They had no choice. They were still puppies and clumsy as all get out.

Daniel was the last to complete his tie in. He was placing the manual inside the knapsack when he accidentally let slip one of the blank diaries. He cursed. It fell, striking several branches, making some noise on its way down. Daniel cringed as one of the lions looked up at where the noise was coming from. It dropped between two of the large cats.

The two cats didn't notice but, the one looking up did. It snapped its head to where the little book slapped quietly into the grass at the trunk of the oak. The massive lioness got up. It leisurely stretched as it was in no particular hurry. It quietly dropped off the lower branch to investigate the fallen object. The lioness could smell the human scent and looked up. Her look of curiosity did not sit well with Daniel or Devin. They looked at each other not knowing what to expect from the giant cat.

Even though they were well hidden, the huge cat caught the subtle movement of the boys at the very top of the tree. It was going to investigate. The lioness compressed its muscles then sprang straight up the oak's great trunk.

As she came, Daniel was uttering ... "Oh shit!! Oh shit!!"

Daniel instructed Devin not to shoot. If they killed the cat, the other lions would eat her as well. The great danger here is that they could only shoot at point blank range in order to hit such a dangerous and fast moving target. None of the boys were skilled at handling such a weapon. They killed the last huge cat with a stationary, unobstructed, point blank shot. What if the next attack came from a cat that would not hesitate but bolt right up and into their midst? A few quick swipes from those massive paws would dislodge the whole group of children from the tree top. She had the power and swiftness to kill them all within seconds. They had never taken down a swift moving target and Daniel doubted seriously that they could ever do so.

The great cat was now some thirty feet up from the ground and then ... hesitated. She turned to look back down at the other giant cats, then, looked up one more time as if contemplating whether it was worth it. She aborted the challenge as she slowly backed down. Devin, Daniel and Jacob loosened the taughtness of their respective bow strings and slowly, silently placed their arrows back in their quivers so as not to arouse the giant cat's curiosity any further. Both took a deep breath.

Several of the big cats yawned and fell back to sleep.

A flock of birds crashed out of that grove of oak trees some seven hundred feet away. Three of the giant cats looked up ... but weren't particularly interested in the squawking birds.

Daniel was looking at the page in Albert's manual that mentioned how to catch birds with a spool of thread. He searched the knapsack and found three spools. This was the safest way to hunt. Not on the ground but ... rather up here, in the trees.

. . .

Albert Morley, on hearing the report of a giant dust devil on the slough in less than one and a half years later, replotted the frequency of the new "events". He tried to verify the reports so that he could be confident that that is what folks around there actually saw. He wasn't disappointed after he learned of the first description of the newest event from a neighbouring farmer. He said it was in July but couldn't remember the exact day. It was around the eighth of July as best as he could remember. Albert was determined to be at the next one. Albert believed that that lightning bolt of some eighteen months ago may have short-circuited all future events by placing them on a new chronology.

In that case, it would be the first winter occurrence of a new event. Albert could expect the next one after that to be in the summer. He tried to contact Eduard. When he did, Eduard was anything but receptive. Eduard simply wanted no more to do with the farms. Manfred made plans to move to Larvyer. The loss of his family was too much. He wanted to forget this place ever existed. Manfred too was not receptive to Albert's overtures to join him to explore the slough further.

All that was soon to change.

As night drew, Manfred found himself sitting in his room in Larvyer, starring out his window, when an idea entered his mind. He sprung bolt upright in his bed, threw his legs over onto the floor and slowly cleared his thoughts.

It was the sixth of July. He chuckled to himself. While he was slowly dipping into a deep depression, Albert was out there going insane. But, he had to admit to himself, that at least Albert was trying to do something about it, however crazy his ideas were.

Manfred suddenly felt a pull to visit Albert. He had heard that he was set up on the old road. Albert had asked him a few days ago to join him. Manfred began to slump back onto his bed but then hesitated. He stared out his window looking across Main Street of the little hamlet of Larvyer, and slowly put the bottle of coke down on the bed side table still staring out the window.

"Damn it!!"

He got up and got dressed. As Manfred was leaving his hotel room, he turned to wave a finger at the mirror hanging by the night table...

"You straighten up right now Manfred Morley. You've got a new mission in life."

He hesitated. He buttoned his shirt, brushed his hair aside and took a deep breath. He had to focus now. He was surprised he had the willpower to do it.

"This is for Gardenia, Dianne and Devin."

He was out the door and stumbled, slightly intoxicated with this new lease on life. He leapt down the hallway to the stairs and out the door. He was finally taking charge of his life once again.

Outside, he took a very deep breath while listening to a little inner voice...

"Steady Manfred ... there's no looking back now."

It was June 29th 1958. The next event was going to happen ... and soon. Albert was waiting. Willie Js. farm had been abandoned. The house was presentable but, empty. If Albert was right, the event should make itself known on precisely the eighth of July. That would clinch it for him. This time, Albert had equipped himself with a 16 mm movie camera with sound, an automatic control and tripod.

Albert was now camped out on Manfred's dusty farm road leading down from the abandoned house to the gravelled municipal road. Albert lived in a makeshift shelter. His camera was always loaded and mounted on a tripod. He waited.

On July sixth, late afternoon, an old truck came up the road from Larvyer. It turned and stopped in front of Albert's shelter. Albert came barrelling out of his tent. He shouted at the driver to move his truck from in front of his shelter, not realizing it was Manfred. Manfred complied.

Albert was stunned as he recognised just who it was. His voice calmed. Albert approached Manfred through the rolled down passenger window.

"What in tar nation brings you out here Manfred?"

Manfred didn't answer. He slipped out of his truck, walked around to the back, went over and stood in front of Albert. Both men looked at each other for a few seconds.

"Albert ... just what do you think you're going to accomplish out here?"

Albert informed Manfred of his theory. Manfred sighed deeply and looked away.

Albert queried ... "What?"

Manfred lowered his head and turned back to look at Albert.

Again Albert asked ... "What?"

Manfred began ... "so you still think this" ... Manfred circled the air with his pinkie ... "giant dust devil with the strange lights is going to make an appearance at exactly on the eighth of July?"

It was Albert's turn to look down and away.

"It has before ... I believe it will again."

For a long time Manfred simply stared at Albert and then slowly turned away softly agreeing with an air of resignation

"Okay...okay...you don't mind me staying here with you...for that ..."

Manfred turned and stretched out his arm to the slough while trying to find the right term ..."event?"

Albert told Manfred it didn't matter one way or the other but, deep down, he was glad to have Manfred's company.

For the next couple days leading up to the eighth of July, Manfred bunked with Albert in the shelter of Albert's tent. Manfred brought what he needed from town, but what he needed most was Albert's company. Though he didn't for a minute believe Albert's story, he secretly wished it were true. It would take his mind off his deep depression and allow him to focus on something, anything in his life that would be worth living for. This was his last ditch attempt at saving himself. After dinner, Albert decided to doze off.

With a deep, deep sigh, Albert stretched back...

"Five hours to midnight" ... he informed Manfred.

"Got to get up at midnight. It'll be the commencement point for the eighth of the July event.
Manfred stretched out on his cot and joined Albert in a deep sleep. Albert's alarm clock went off at midnight. There was a full moon in the sky lighting up everything underneath it in a pale blue light.

"This was it", thought Albert ..."It's now or never".

In the middle of the night, Albert rushed around like a man on fire. He positioned the tripod about twenty feet from their shared tent just off the shoulder of the municipal road. Manfred was still asleep on his sleeping bag. Albert yelled at Manfred to come out.

"Was the event under way?" Manfred thought.

He leapt out of his bag and scurried quickly out of the tent. He approached Albert.

"Why don't you take the first watch ..." Albert instructed Manfred.

He provided Manfred with a chair. If anything were to happen, Manfred was to yell at Albert. Albert stayed dressed so that no time would be wasted in getting out there. Within three hours, Albert could still not sleep. He was worried about Manfred staying awake. As he got up to look outside, Manfred's head was buried deep in his chest. Albert wasn't angry. He understood what Manfred was going through. So, typical of Albert, he brought Manfred out a cup of coffee from his thermos, a second chair and sat beside him. He nudged Manfred awake.

Manfred woke with a start, apologetic to Albert about the possibility that he may have missed the event. Albert reassured him that he had not. He couldn't sleep. Together, they talked into the early morning light. Both men took turns to relieve themselves. By seven o'clock in the early morning, they were somewhat awake. They could sleep deeply tonight.

Manfred was walking back and forth on the road. He lit a cigarette, trying to blot out the sharp urge to go back to town. Four more excruciatingly long hours had passed. Manfred felt he was dying. For a moment, he thought he could hear Albert. A second later Manfred jumped as Albert touched his shoulder.

"I said ... we've got just one more hour Manfred. It always happens at noon hour precisely ... except last year. I don't think it came."

He quickly added to reassure Manfred...

"But I hear someone else did see it that day".

Albert winked and headed back to the standing tripod.

"If you say so Albert," Manfred uttered, "If you say so ..."

A couple of mallard ducks glided down in tight formation onto the now wet slough. This time the slough had turned into a marshland thanks to the rains. He watched the two birds splash into Morley Lake. He could see a tractor in the far distance, on what used to be his land, the land he and Gardenia called home, the land that he and Gardenia were to raise their first family together. He had lost everything.

Albert noticed the look in Manfred's eyes. Here was a young nephew of his contemplating what might have been. He faced Manfred directly and told him to take a hike ... literally. Manfred needed to be alone in his thoughts. He asked Albert if it was okay to do so.

Albert reassured him...

"Go ... go."

He smiled at Manfred. Manfred looked at Albert and nodded. Manfred took off and walked half way around Morley Lake then turned around to come back. He looked at Albert from a distance.

"My god", Manfred thought.
"Albert was really taking this personally". He admired Albert.

Albert in the meantime thought the walk would do Manfred a lot of good. He would be more relaxed when he came back ... get a few things out of his system.

It was closing in on "Event-Day" very rapidly. Manfred had walked back to within three hundred feet of Albert. Albert ignored him while looking nervously at his watch. Barely three minutes to go. This was it. Everything in the past year and a half was for this very moment. Manfred was within one hundred fifty feet of Albert. Sixty seconds to go. Albert was totally focussed. He leaned forward into the camera's eye piece. He looked at his watch. Nine seconds to go. Manfred looked at his. He was seventy five feet from Albert and abruptly stopped. His gaze was transfixed on the watershed. His heart was pounding.

He was taking deep breaths.

Albert counted down ... "3 ... 2 ... 1 ..."

"E – DAY"

THE ESCAPE

Georgi looked at Daniel in astonishment.

"That's the plan?"

Daniel didn't answer or turn away from Georgi's gaze.

"...With those monsters out there?"

Daniel still didn't say anything. He was hoping it was a good plan that everybody could agree on.

"With those monsters out there...?" Georgi queried once again.

"Georgi," Daniel started, "we can't stay here. We need water and food. We need to build a base camp where we can cook and sleep safely. We can never get down from here with those giant cats blocking our survival. Do you understand that?"

Georgi looked away with a heavy sigh. He knew Daniel was right. The plan had to be executed with precision if any of them were going to survive. They could still all die. But, if they stayed here, death was almost certain. Every dilemma they found themselves in always ended up as a life or death scenario. He looked around. All eyes were upon him. If anyone had another plan, he was waiting to hear it. He looked around one last time. Nobody responded. So, the plan went ahead, as scary as it was.

With one of the diaries, Jacob was to record the movement of each lion's whereabouts. The older children believed that these monster cats hunted as a pride. From their vantage point, they could easily make out where members of the pride ventured and how far away they travelled from the oak. The children had barely two days worth of Beef Jerky left, thanks to the discovery that Gordon had hidden about eight packages and forgot about them in the bottom of his knapsack. They could wait out the lions for another two days possibly three. Concealment was getting hazardous as children wanted to get up and move around.

Over the next two days, the giant cats were getting a whiff of the excrement being dropped by the kids from the trees. Albert's diary even covered the situation of wiping themselves with broad-leafed vegetation. They were going to get into dire straights soon. Their canteens of water were now empty. This was going to get very unpleasant. It was going to reach a do or die situation and they were going to weaken as each day passed.

Late in the evening of that day, the first indication that they could no longer stay where they were was nearly upon them. The sky overhead had grown dark, very dark. This was very ominous and perhaps as dangerous a scenario as facing the entire pride of big cats. The air cooled dramatically.

This is what Daniel most feared. Jacob, Beverly, Benny, Georgi and Devin gathered around to discuss the impending danger. The intermittent flashes of lightning and rumble of thunder heralded a massive storm. The branches were now blowing and the tree began to sway. Beverly agreed to watch over and comfort Vera, Di-Di and Gordon. The puppies will help in this sense.

The children were straddled up four levels of branches. Di-Di, Vera and Gordon occupied the top tier with lots of branches above them to shield them. The second and third tiers were occupied by Beverly, Georgi and Benny. The bottom tier was occupied by the bow hunters Devin, Jacob and Daniel.

An enormous flash of light lit up the tree, followed three seconds later by an ear shattering bang that made them all jump. The children yelled. The puppies began whimpering. It was important to stay with the three little ones in case they became hysterical with fear and alert the curiosity of the big cats. Daniel, Benny and

Georgi climbed up and down to reassure everyone that they were all safe. The older ones were worried about a fatal lightning strike that would kill them all but there was nothing anyone could do. Another brilliant flash of light told everyone that they were going to have their bones rattled ... again. It came ... two seconds later. It was another ear shattering bang.

Then ... Nature struck them hard with hail. This, they hadn't counted upon. Everyone was yelling. It was absolute mayhem. The puppies began to yelp. At least they were staying in their knapsacks. The hail smashed through the dense foliage and hit the branches and kids. It was going to be a very rough night. Beverly, Georgi and Devin threw themselves on the little ones to protect them and quiet them.

But it was too late. Vera panicked and had loosened her ropes and had squirmed out of them. She then lost her grip on the slippery wet branch and slid off. Beverly grabbed at her and caught the little girl by the wrist. She was flailing and screaming below the branch some forty five feet above the giant cats huddled below.

The crescendo of hail all but blotted out her screams. If the big cats heard her above the crashing hailstones ... they didn't care. Hail was quite disagreeable with them as well. Devin swung under the branch and grabbed her by the ankle as she slipped out of Beverly's grasp. Devin was losing his grip on the tree. Jacob did a four-legged scramble out on his branch to grab his little sister as Devin completely lost his grip and fell with both he and Vera's tiny body plummeting past Jacob. He was horror struck as his little sister fell. Jacob was only able to just grab Devin by his left hand as his cousin fell past him clinging to Vera's ankle with his other hand. Jacob wrapped his legs around the branch as tightly as he could.

Beverly scrambled down while yelling at Georgi and Benny to keep the little ones covered. She did a dog crawl out to the branch where Jacob lay gripping Devin's hand. Vera was screaming, dangling upside down. Devin had an iron grip on her. Their position was precarious. At any moment, one of the lions could look up ... and it would be all over for the group. The hail was the only thing muffling Vera's screams. The hail could stop at any moment exposing them all. Beverly grabbed at Georg's wrist. Together they began to pull Devin back up yelling at him not to drop Vera. As Georg scrambled slowly over Jacob, Beverly grabbed little Vera. She was still screaming.

Then the hail suddenly stopped.

Jacob yelled at Devin to "Go! Go!"

One of the big cats stirred. It lifted its head. Soon, all the cats began to stir. As soon as Beverly grabbed Vera, she snapped her hand quickly around Vera's mouth, shushing her to stop screaming.

She whispered into Vera's ear...

"...The lions! The lions! You're safe Vera! You're safe!"

Everyone froze as the big cats began to look around. Vera was safe and whimpering softly. She had had a very, very close call. Beverly took the little girl up to her perch from which she previously fell.

Jacob motioned Devin and Daniel to slip down a few branches to see what the giant cats were up to. Lightning flashes lit up the tree and surrounding area allowing the boys to see the big cats nestled below. The next lightning flash exposed the lower branches. What they didn't see put them on immediate guard.

They didn't see the cats at all. They were gone. Where were they? They wouldn't have climbed higher into the tree. In the next lightning flash Devin was the first to notice a tail from one of the monster cats' twitch from under the enormous lower branches. The cats had sought shelter, on the ground under the bottom branches. It was pouring rain. Still lightning. Now only rolls of thunder reverberated across the dark, inky, black sky with lightning lighting up their new world, keeping them abreast of what was happening below them. The kids were calmer, if just a little wet. It was going to be a cold miserable night but, at least, they had each others' bodily heat to cling to.

The following morning, damp and shivering, the boys on the lower branches noticed that the lions were back up on their perches.
Jacob was the first to notice. One of the lions, the one with the arrow shaft in its shoulder was gone. It was crouching down in the grass. Two other lions had left as well, to investigate the injured cat. The wounded lioness and the two other female cats who investigated her were probably siblings. They stood guard over her. They were sending a clear message to the rest of the pride that she was not to be attacked. All the giant cats seemed to be getting restless.

The children had been up in the crown of the oak now for nearly three days. Beverly was the first to observe from her vantage point that the two very large half tonne males had simultaneously risen and quietly dropped off their perch. The rest of the pride followed.

The pride of monster cats was on the move.

One of the knapsacks had a pair of binoculars in it. Devin ever so carefully put the strap around his neck. They were quite heavy. He was having trouble focussing. Jacob and Bud were still keeping an eye on the two big males of the pride.

They were now some fifty yards out into the grasslands. The rest of the pride was following. Daniel was trying to see through the foliage. Strange. The direction they were going was opposite that of the waterway lined with the fifty oaks.

It was then that Daniel had spotted what looked like very large camels in the distance, five of them at least. About two hundred yards to the left of the camels were a herd of horses. All were grazing while the camels were in a grove of trees browsing on the foliage. The way was clear for an escape from their oak prison. The pride by now, judging by the movement in the grasses, was at least a quarter mile away. Everybody was packed up and ready to

go. The descent had to be careful but rapid. The extra focus and movement by the child explorers warmed them up. It was getting exciting. No one knew how long the pride was going to be out.
If they killed something, they would stay and eat it at the kill site. The big cats may stay out longer if they miss their quarry, but everybody would be betting their lives on it. The adrenaline was building once again.

As they began their decent, Beverly noticed that there were only six trails left by the departure of the monster cats. She instinctively stopped and shouted down to the lead group of boys descending the great oak.

"Daniel! Jake! Devin!"

All three boys froze. The boys turned to look back up.

"Guys! There are only six trails out there. Where are the other three?" Beverly yelled.

Daniel turned and looked back down anxiously.

Jacob yelled back up to them ... "Maybe a couple of the cats might be just following in the path of some of the others of their pride. It would make sense in the tall grass. Right?"

For a few brief moments everyone hesitated. Jacob then motioned everyone to continue their decent.

The children with their puppies were near the base of the first massive bottom branches. Devin, Daniel and Jacob leapt upon the lowest branch from where Devin and Benny had slain their first monster cat. All three boys snatched an arrow from their quivers and placed it on their respective bows. They drew the bow strings back tightly and pointed their weapons in the direction the massive lions had headed out. They whispered loudly for the children to climb down off the last branch. Beverly was the first down peering under the bottom massive branches. No lions. She grabbed each of the little ones first.

Benny and Georgi followed. No movement came from the grass around the oak. Devin climbed down next. Jacob was about to sheath his arrow when Daniel called out...

"Not yet Jake! Wait 'til Devin rearms his weapon. Okay... now!"

Jacob was on the ground in six seconds, turned and rearmed his bow with an arrow. Daniel was down on the ground ten seconds after Jacob. All three were now rearmed and cautiously backed up to rejoin the others.

Beverly, Georgi and Benny carried the three spears. They were on their way once again. They had to move fast. They had a good lead in time on the big cats. They were half way there already. The puppies were still fairly quiet.

The three child bow hunters had prematurely relaxed their bow strings when the boys heard the rustle of grasses behind them, forcing them to spin around in sheer terror, drawing their bow strings back taught. Their hearts skipped a beat. They could hear heavy breathing. They could see the top of the body of one of the lionesses'. She was terrifyingly big. Then ... she toppled over onto her side. The heavy breathing stopped. She was less than ten feet away. The arrow head lodged deeply in the big cat had taken its toll. She crumpled to the ground.

The boys closed in. They had to be sure despite Daniel's loud objections to the contrary that the great cat may not be dead.

"You guys!!! The other lionesses that were with her could still be here!!! Don't be idiots!!!"

Devin, without taking his eyes off the now reposed lioness, declared ... "They would have left to hunt with the others".

Daniel knew somehow that that did make sense. Jacob looked back in the direction the big cat had come from. Nothing stirring in the grass. All three waited for an attack that never materialized ... and that was good.

The other children had stopped and were waiting for the boys. The boys quickly regrouped and the children continued their safari to the giant grove. Within five minutes, they had entered the grove with some relief. They had found a tree, easy to climb with the lower branches only eight feet from the ground and whose massive trunk was a little back from the water's edge by about sixty feet.

It was a slightly spread out oasis of broad-leafed oaks along a stream bed whose banks were not more than thirty to forty feet wide. It felt like home.

DOLL HOUSE

The grasslands extended into, around and through the grove of trees. The giant cats were left well behind the child explorers, though this grassland was still within the domain of these monsters. It was still their territory. Here, the grove of trees extended on both sides of the little stream bed ... its watery course winding its way through the oak dominated grove within a mini-forest of spruce trees.

Daniel, Jacob and Devin surveyed this tiny woodland. Plenty of building materials for a tree house surrounded the little group of children. One of the knapsacks even had a small hand-axe attached to it. Jacob started to gather everyone together. He had everybody assigned to a task. They had to complete this before nightfall or they would all be sitting out in the rain once more and nobody wanted that.

The little ones in the group were still cold and hungry. Di-Di and Vera were both crying that their tummies hurt. Even the pups were whining. So Daniel promised Vera and Di-Di that, by tonight, they would eat their first hot meal.

"Would you like to help us build you a house to live in?" Daniel said matter-of-factly.

They nodded in unison as Beverly wiped the tears from their little faces. Gordon was also having trouble containing the gnawing hunger. It was a tall order for all of them but, they had to try. Daniel and Jacob were now familiar with how to make hemp, a kind of rope, thanks to Uncle Albert. They could also use the hemp to create a makeshift floor by tying together branches for their tree house if they were careful.

And so it began.

Beverly volunteered to organize the three youngest children into a search party to gather up three sizes of kindling for a fire. Beverly was given Devin's bow and quiver to protect the four of them. Jacob, Georgi and Benny were to chop branches, all the same size into ten foot lengths. One of the boys was to tear long strips of bark from the old rotted trunks of trees lying about on the forest floor. This was the hemp with which the older children would attempt to tie the ten foot branches together. Jacob carried the second bow.

Georgi and Benny carried two of the three spears that Uncle Albert had fashioned for them. Daniel carried the third bow while Devin carried the third spear. They were the hunters.

Daniel remembered the flock of birds that flew out from one of these oaks high in the crown of the tree.

"Those birds were potential food" ... he thought.

No one knew how far they would get before nightfall but at least they will have a fire. There was a tin of dry wooden matches in one of the ruck sacks. They had to be used sparingly. They had yet to learn how to make a real fire despite the fact that Uncle Albert had wrapped the kindling mechanism in a cloth pouch. The children still had a lot to learn. They were still alive if just barely, thanks to fierce survival instincts. It would be some time before experience kicked in. They faced early annihilation if it didn't kick in soon enough. The older boys and Beverly tried not to think about it.

It was still morning. The children felt their spirits lift as they slowly began to take control of their lives in this new world. They were adapting quickly. Sheer necessity drove them to innovate. The children were ignoring their hunger. They were focused now on multidisciplinary tasks. They were learning new things driven by their instinct to survive.

 By noon hour, Beverly's little crew had three enormous piles of kindling around their oak tree. They kept going. Jacob's three-child crew had piled some twenty five branches by the oak, ten foot pieces each. Daniel had climbed up and into their oak tree and cross-threaded a large spool of thread like a giant spider web in amongst the smaller branches. He was setting a trap. He hoped it would work.

He climbed back down. He and Devin then proceeded to the bank of the small stream and dipped the canteens into the slowly moving water. Daniel stood watch as Devin filled the canteens.

There was a small sandy island upstream about five hundred feet with quite a few logs lying scattered across it. Daniel thought of exploring it later. He looked down at Devin filling the last of the canteens. At least they'll have fresh water for their little base camp. Another two minutes passed before Devin was finished. They packed up the canteens to haul back up the oak tree.

Devin looked upstream and pointed to a barren sandy island upon which they could cross if they had to get to the other side of the grasslands. Daniel looked up. His heart skipped a beat. The logs were gone from on top of that sand bar.

"Where the hell were the tree trunks?" Daniel thought.

Jacob, Georgi and Benny had piled ten foot branches about the base of the oak. They were hauling 1 up at a time into the higher branches. The kids found an ideal area about thirty feet up the tree that was criss-crossed with many of the oaks supporting branches. It was dangerously close to the ground. After the floor had been laid out, it was bound together with the crudely produced hemp. It worked. By early afternoon, the three older children not only had the floor finished, but now had another thirty branches gathered. These they did not strip of leaves but left them on, complete with smaller branches. They were now tying the ends of these branches to their crude floor. They had successfully assembled for themselves, what might be called a two-sided six foot high triangular shelter about ten feet long by ten feet wide. It was small but adequate. The leafy branches covering the two-sided lean-to made it all but invisible up in the great oak.

In the interim, Daniel and Devin headed back up to the spider web snare, set from the spool of thread that they had set high in their oak tree. There was some fluttering of wings. They had made a catch, several in fact.

As Devin was about to climb to retrieve them ... he stopped. He asked Daniel about the idea of creating hooks so that they may be able to fish. Daniel retorted that Albert had created wooden hooks with apparently some small feathers attached to them. Albert had five in all stashed away in a tiny tackle box. Daniel was going to look at them tonight. He was dying to try them out.

Daniel climbed up after Devin. They had ensnared five beautiful waxwings. They were about the size of crows, grey in color with a touch of burgundy and white about their heads. Both boys stood there on the branch admiring the birds.

"Now what?" Daniel asked.

"We grab them and kill them." Devin retorted.

Daniel didn't like that idea at all but, it was either eat or starve. There was no way around it.

"...How?" Daniel inquired.

"We cut their heads off killing them instantly then ... we pluck them ... just like chickens" Devin stated matter of factly.

Daniel had to fight the urge to throw up. "Where do we do ... this?"

But Devin was already doing it. He handed the first headless fluttering bird to his older cousin. Blood was spraying everywhere. Daniel's heart was racing. He looked up at the horizon. He had to steady himself. He didn't want to appear squeamish in front of his younger cousin.

The boys tied the five dead birds to one of the branches high in their tree. Daniel thought ... "It might be unwise to do so."

Both boys climbed down the tree and joined their cousins. When they climbed back down to what was their newly if crudely built home in the large oak, they were utterly surprised by the enterprise. It had worked.

The younger kids were hoisted up into the tree house some thirty feet off the ground which they christened ... "Doll House". The older kids, hungry and tired, continued to build a second shelter at the base of the oak, on the ground. The second shelter was smaller and protected their kindling from rain. They placed it directly under one of the oak's massive lower limbs. It was constructed in the form of a tepee. It too was covered by leafy branches to keep it somewhat waterproof. Some of the kindling was taken up the oak and into the open back end of their shelter. Three heavy logs were also brought up.

By nightfall, the older boys had put their birds on a spit over an enclosed fire whose amber glow made for a very comfortable evening. Daniel was determined that they were going to eat better tomorrow night. It was either fish or some mammal. It didn't matter which. Although they were all still hungry, the sharp edge was taken off. They shared the roast birds among themselves and the three little puppies who were starting to teethe. What no one had realised was that the scent of cooked flesh was now wafting over the grasslands. But that aside, it was quiet inside the lean-to.

Everyone was supremely satisfied, even beaming, over their accomplishments. They were going to survive after all. If they thought this was a guarantee, they were wrong.

That night, they all stretched out on the leafy branches in their lean-to and fell pleasantly to sleep. Devin and Jacob kept watch with their spears and bows at the ready.

The bird bones and feathers had all simply been thrown into the fire, less they acquire unwanted quests during the night. For the very first time they caught a breather to actually discuss how they all got here in this strange yet familiar world. There were no answers of course, just questions and unsubstantiated ideas born of children's wild, unfettered imaginations. For breakfast tomorrow, they had an iron pot to boil eggs in ... if they could find some nests in the tree tops.

BACKYARD TERROR

The next morning, the children were up at the crack of dawn. The older boys and Beverly discussed the idea of constructing another shelter over top the one they already built as added insurance in case the weather turned ugly, a hail guard of sorts. Beverly wanted the little ones to stay put. She would stay with them and keep their attention off the fact that they were most probably never going to see their parents again.

Jacob, Benny and Georgi headed out to gather more branches. This was going to be a little easier. Within a couple of hours, they were hauling the branches up the tree above their shelter. Their new structure was a lean-to with no bottom.

By noon, the secondary structure was complete. Daniel and Devin spent about an hour and a half climbing oaks and retrieving birds' eggs. They now had sixteen eggs in all, each the size of small chicken eggs. A few times, they had to fight off the parents guarding those nests. Devin was collecting them in a small tin pot. It was precarious. They moved slowly and by some miracle managed not to break any.

Once back and up into their makeshift shelter, they built a fire, emptied one of the thermoses of its water and proceeded to boil the eggs. It was a lot of precarious work for just over a dozen eggs.

After breakfast, they were going to go fishing. Fish would be an added variety to their meals. The wooden hooks that Henry provided were tied with string wound around the middle of a piece of wood no longer than six inches or so.

"Guess you're supposed to hold onto that while the hook was in the water" Daniel thought.

"You know ..." Beverly began "... you guys could climb out on the lower branches of this tree and drop your line from there. It's not far above the water ... maybe eight feet ..."

Daniel looked out across the branch and then at Devin. It was a great idea. Daniel measured the length of the fine fishing line that Henry had installed. It was about twelve feet in length. Devin had climbed out on one of the lower branches of their oak tree and had dipped the fine thirty pound-test line into the water from above. Earlier, they had dug up a worm and placed it on the hook. It didn't take long.

Jacob, Georgi and Benny were at the base of the oak looking at the neatly stacked piles of kindling in the lean-to compound figuring out how better to stack the wood when a strange feeling brushed against Jacob's psyche. He slowly turned and peered across the landscape. He had caught something out of the corner of his eye earlier ... in the distance while collecting wood for the structure. He scanned the horizon again. It was about one of those spruce trees some three hundred feet away. He focussed on it and wandered a few yards away from the boys, placing his hands on his hips and stopped to stare at the spruce trees in the distance.

He saw something when he was collecting branches with the other boys. It was only for a moment that he had glanced at it. But he remembered. He called out to the other boys to stay where they were. They glanced at him for a moment then concentrated on re-arranging the stockpile of kindling. Jacob was still motionless standing only about 10 feet away.

"It's probably nothing" he reassured himself.

But the feeling bothered him like a nasty mosquito bite he had to scratch.

A large carp grabbed at the bait and was hooked. It was probably twenty pounds. It fought as Devin reined it in.

"This is going to be a great meal" he thought.

He could see the fish under water. As it splashed to the surface, Devin was having quite the time attempting to haul it up. Daniel hurried along the branch to give Devin a hand. He was looking down into the water when a large shadow seemed to float up behind and underneath the fish.

Devin struggled to lift the fish just three feet above the water, dismissing the shadow as a disturbed log. Daniel crouched down on the branch to help lift the fish up. Neither one paid any attention to the massive shadow twitching violently from side to side while picking up speed like a vertically fired torpedo heading swiftly to the surface directly under their branch.

It was huge.

The boys were too focused on getting their prize, fighting against the glare of sunlight scattering off the water's surface, dangling precariously over each side of the oak's branch.

Both boys recoiled in complete terror as the log under their carp opened wide ... exposing massive teeth while simultaneously launching itself straight up out of the water towards the branch that the two boys were fishing from ... slamming its great jaws shut with a resounding crash only inches from them, soaking the boys with the spray.

Their fish had disappeared down a monstrous pinkish gullet. The eyes of the huge two thousand pound blackish green and yellowish reptile met theirs on the branch some thirteen feet up from the water before slipping back down with an enormous splash. The two boys were left breathless and gasping, trying to regain their composure. Both, with great haste, backed away from their fishing spot. Beverly stuck her head out from the lean-to.

"... I heard a huge splash guys ... catch anything or did one of you fall in?" she laughed.

She immediately noticed the serious expressions on the face of the two boys. Beverly looked at the two boys...

"What?"

Devin looked up at Beverly ... "It damn near caught us!"

"What are you blubbering on about?" Beverly asked quizzically.

"Hey! You guys!" came the shout from below.

"Did you guys see that?" Georgi called up to the boys.

"Yah, we were almost inside it!" Devin sputtered back.

"Inside what?" Beverly asked.

"...A huge crocodile!" Devin retorted.

"...A huge what?" Beverly asked incredulously.

Daniel then instructed Beverly to keep the small kids away from the ends of the branches overlooking the small river and made sure that everyone was alerted to the possibility that these large reptilian predators could be in the grasses surrounding their oak tree.

"As if we don't have enough to worry about"... Daniel thought.

He even wondered if their arrows would have any effect on those armoured hides. They may have to depend almost exclusively on their spears for protection.

Devin looked around the base of the oak tree from his perch off the ground.

"Benny! Georgi! Where's Jake?"

The boys below both pointed to a group of trees some three hundred feet away from their oak.

Daniel yelled down ..."You guys are to stay together! At all times! I don't have to tell you how dangerous it is out here!"

Georgi was a little annoyed and shouted back "Jacob told us it was alright! He told us to stay."

Georgi rolled his eyes and looked at Benny ... "Sheesh..."

Daniel was down on the ground in seconds and facing Benny and Georgi.

"You guys come with me. Show me where he is."

Reluctantly, the two boys went with Daniel.

"Jesus guys! ... Never, ever break up your group. Benny? Georgi?"

Benny turned away ..."Okay Daniel okay."

Now Benny was getting annoyed. But the lesson had to be reiterated. As the little troop of kids slipped through the tall grass, Daniel spotted Jacob some three hundred feet away just standing there looking up at a spruce tree. He was just standing there. He seemed spooked.

SOMETHING TO LIVE FOR

As the little group approached Jacob, they slowed their pace.

Daniel called out softly...

"Jacob?"

Jacob put his hand up palm open. Everyone froze. Daniel slowly drew an arrow from his quiver and placed it on his bow. Jacob motioned them with a closed fist with a bobbing forward pointing finger to approach quietly, slowly. When the little troop reached Jacob, Daniel whispered

"What is it ... Jacob?"

There was no response. He whispered again...

"Jacob ... what's the matter? What's happening?"

Jacob did not speak or make a sound or even turn around to acknowledge their presence but kept his gaze on one area high in the tree top.

"Jacob. This is serious. What the hell are you spooked about? This isn't funny" ... Daniel whispered again and more harshly this time.

Then it was Jacob's turn to whisper ... and it was becoming a little electrifying.

"Daniel. Do you see it? Up in the tree?"

By now Benny, Georgi and Daniel were all straining to see something up in the tree.

"Is it moving?" ...Daniel was thinking of a possible panther.

"No."... Jacob quietly shot back.

Jacob slowly raised his arm and pointed to the object high in the tree top ... The thing was sitting nearly half way up in the hundred foot spruce tree.

"Do you see it? It's the same colour as the tree. It's big and it ain't moving. It's just sitting there. It's nearly half way up ... close to the top of the tree." Jacob stated.

Each of the boys began to notice that something was indeed out of place high in the crown of the spruce. Whatever it was ... the thing sitting up there ... quietly ... was really big.

"Benny! Can you climb up to get a good look at that thing up there?" Jacob suggested.

"What if it attacks me?" Benny shot back.

"I don't think it will." Georgi interjected.

Daniel and Jacob turned to Georgi.

"Why not...?" Daniel asked.

"Because ... I think we're looking at some sort of structure."... Georgi whispered.

"That's what I think too Georgi. It's some sort of platform. I think someone could be on it."... Jacob shot back.

Daniel was astonished. "You guys think someone else is out here with us?" ... he said.

"Only one way to find out" ... Benny said with bravado as he began to climb "Gimme a push, someone."

Daniel and Georgi boosted Benny up by their hands ... and he was away.

"Careful Ben..." Daniel whispered.

As Benny climbed, he noticed small sticks had been imbedded into the tree trunk. One was broken. Someone had built a very crude but effective ladder right into the trunk of the Spruce. As Benny climbed, a group of waxwings burst out from the tree tops. His heart skipped a beat. He knew, if anyone was there, they had now been alerted. He froze and waited. He was still some twenty five to thirty feet under the structure which itself was some fifty feet up in the hundred foot spruce tree.

It was a platform alright. No one, he hoped, was home. He continued his rapid ascent towards the structure. He was now just twelve feet underneath the platform. He slowly climbed up to and just under the branch that supported this structure when he froze in horror. Something or someone had moved on the platform. A couple of dried leaves fell away from the other side of the structure. Benny was now terrified. He had no where to go. He wanted to turn and shout for help ... shout to the guys below that someone was here. The boys below could see their cousin had stopped. They decided not to distract him ... not to encourage him to go any further if his safety was jeopardised.

Benny turned his gaze back to the well hidden platform. There was more movement on top of the structure. He had no weapon with him. He would be utterly helpless if attacked. His cousins and brother had no clear shot from their position some forty to fifty feet below. Too much foliage. He now wished the hell he hadn't volunteered in his enthusiasm to be the first to see what was up there in the spruce tree. This sucked ... big time. His heart was pounding as to who was going to see who first.

He took a deep breath as he ever so slowly began to slide his leg over that last and final branch. The structure was only some ten feet out from the trunk of the tree and spread between two large branches. This was it ... all the marbles brought into play. With one arm and one leg over the branch, he slowly pulled himself up and around. The platform came alive with activity as a cloud of leaves burst up from the base and a snarling demon from hell threw itself off the platform and down the branch at Benny. Benny's eyes opened wide as saucers as he let out a bloodcurdling scream 50 feet up in the tree.

. . .

Albert was still looking through the aperture of his camera. Manfred's gaze was still transfixed on the marshlands of the Morley slough. Neither one of them moved. A minute went by as Albert began licking his lips in anticipation. Manfred, who was some seventy five feet from Albert, turned to look at him. Albert hadn't budged. He was still focused. After three minutes, Albert slowly looked up and fixed his gaze on the marshland. Manfred sighed deeply and started to walk over to Albert. Albert stood up, bit his lower lip and placed his hands on his hips. He was blinking hard in incomprehension as he turned to address Manfred who walked up beside him. He shrugged his shoulders.

"I don't get it. Maybe the timing of this thing is way off somehow. Maybe the energy from that lightning bolt ... aaaahh ... who am I kidding..."

Albert took a deep breath then, lowered his head in disappointment. It was palpable.

Manfred placed his hand on Albert's shoulder...

"...Can't say you didn't try Albert."

Manfred turned slowly and walked back to his truck taking one last look at the marshland. His kids were gone and there was nothing left for either one of them to do but accept it.

Manfred headed back into town, parked his truck and went into the hotel bar. A few Native Indians and a couple of tourists just passing through on a hunting trip were the sole customers there. He ordered lunch and for the first time in a very long time, Manfred ordered a tall coke with ice. He began to realise that it was better to be crazy like Albert than depressed 24/7.

Yet, deep down, he never thought Albert was even the slightest bit uncorked.

As Manfred quietly ate his lunch and reflected on the last three days with Albert, he began to chuckle to himself.

"Talk about two crazy guys, sitting out on a municipal road waiting for some ludicrous miracle to occur. So this is what its all come down to. After the loss of my family, they'll think I ended up in the loony bin ..." Manfred thought to himself. At least Albert will be keeping me company."

Manfred continued to eat breakfast, toast, eggs, bacon and a coffee with a glass of coke. Somehow he felt better. The door creaked open and old man Willard walked in.

The little cow bell rang as the door slammed shut again. He saw Manfred.

"How the hell are you Mannie? Haven't seen or heard from you in months!"

Manfred greeted Willard politely. They shook hands.

Willard said softly ... "If there's anything Lilith and I can do ..."

"It's alright Willard. I'm doing just fine."

"No he wasn't" ... he thought to himself.

"Listen. Why don't you come over for dinner tonight? Lilith will set another plate out. We haven't had much company in a while" ... Willard invited.

"Thanks Willard. I've had a rough three days and only want to sleep early tonight. Been out with Albert on that ... damn slough looking for some silly stuff ..."

Manfred waved his hand and picked up his coffee.

"Can I grab you a coffee Willard?"

Willard didn't answer but abruptly changed the topic.

"What silly stuff Mannie?"

"Oh ... you know ... some dust devil that has all these coloured lights that's supposed to appear every year and a half ... according to Albert."

Manfred started to chuckle again. It was funny actually. He enjoyed his short time with his Uncle Albert. He felt like a kid again. Life wasn't so bad. Willard spoke up...

"I was the one who saw it, Mannie. On your farm, on your homestead."

Manfred slowly looked up incredulously.

"You saw what Willard? What did you see?"

Willard rose from Manfred's table

"IT! I saw IT ... with my own eyes."

Willard poked two fingers towards his eyes...

"Albert isn't the only one."

Manfred looked at Willard ... "You're the one who told Albert?"

Willard didn't answer as the door creaked open with the bell ringing announcing four more visitors arriving into the restaurant. Willard excused himself saying he was meeting with a few business friends. He would see Manfred later.

Manfred couldn't put it away. "When did you see it?"

Willard hesitated ... "about a year and a half ago on January eighth ... give or take".

"Do you remember the time Willard?" Manfred shot back.

Willard scratched his head as if digging for the correct answer...

"I think I remember now ... yes ... yes ... I remember now checking my watch ... yes I do remember that now. It was three o'clock in the afternoon. Funny. I couldn't remember that up until now."

Manfred looked at his watch. He had been in the restaurant for over two hours reading the newspaper along with his breakfast. Manfred fired back...

"Are you absolutely sure it was three o'clock?"

"Yes. Three o'clock..." Willard retorted.

Manfred looked at his watch again and dug into his pocket for a few dollars and threw it on the table.

"Thanks Willard ... you've been a big help!" Manfred called back as he left the restaurant in a full run.

The door banged open and Manfred was gone.

"Uh ... Okay... Mannie ..."

Willard stated quietly, standing alone as he watched Manfred through the window running for his truck.

Manfred headed over to the Larvyer Railroad station on the corner of the main drag.

There was a phone in there. He tried to phone Albert, but there was no answer. Maybe he's on his way home? No. He wouldn't leave. Not today. Knowing Albert's avocation for this ... thing, Albert would most likely stay on the site 'til next morning.

It was eighteen minutes to three o'clock. As Manfred's pick-up roared down the main drag, he passed Larvyer's only gas station which forced him to take a glance at his fuel gauge. It registered empty.

"Damn! Damn! Damn!" ... as Manfred pounded his fist against the steering wheel...

"...Why now!?!"

He spun his pick-up around, headed back past the Barclay Hotel and pulled up to get gas at the brick factory. Eddy Wesley, the old gas attendant came out and went to the gas cap on Manfred's vehicle.

"Damn! Can't he go a little faster...like today?"

Manfred was impatient. Eddy filled the tank. Manfred gave him seven dollars.

"Wait here"... Eddy replied, "I'll get your change."

"Keep it!" Manfred shouted, and he was away.

A quick look at his watch told him he had seven minutes. He could be there in five. He pushed the accelerator to the metal and rocketed up from Larvyer on the valley floor straining to reach the top of the valley and open prairie. He turned off and onto a side road off the main highway. It was rolling hills with only room for one vehicle. Slowing down to pass was treacherous. A small yawning canyon graced the side between Manfred's vehicle and the main highway. It was heavily treed. Roll off the road and into the canyon and nobody would find you for days. The other side was a steep cutback into the side of the hill. Manfred's farm was the first on the right hand side, and there, was Albert's equipment ... still standing near the side of the road. Manfred pulled up to where he left Albert.

Everything was still there. Albert hadn't taken anything down. But where the hell was Albert? Manfred looked at his watch one more time. His vehicle ground to a halt behind the tripod. Eighty seconds to go.

"Where the dickens is he?"

Manfred couldn't believe that Albert ... for one moment would abandon this gear. He leapt from his truck and ran into the tent. No Albert. He called out. No answer. Manfred was turning round and round, jerking his body around this way and that, to look for Albert.

"This makes no sense." Manfred thought.

He stopped. He started to laugh.

"What's going to happen?"

He spread his arms out wide.

"The heavens are going to open up and a chorus of angels blowing trumpets were going to appear?" Manfred said out loud to himself.

He couldn't stop laughing at how spooked Albert had made him.

"I sure have the giggles today" he thought. "I raced all the way up here? And for what, to be a little kid again with Albert?"

Manfred couldn't stop laughing. The joke was on him and he had taken the bait.

"Let's see now ..." Manfred stated as he reached into his pocket and grabbed a nickel.

"Heads ... I start banging my head on the hood of my truck."

Manfred was giggling so much he almost started to stagger.

"Tails ... I turn both myself and Albert in for psychiatric care."

In that one single moment as Manfred tossed the nickel straight up into the air, it arced in a curve and flew away over his shoulder towards the marsh. It vanished. His teeth were also aching. It was the fillings. He grabbed his mouth and at the same time whipped around to follow the path of his nickel as it flew towards the marsh and disappeared into...

Manfred faced the marsh in utter astonishment.

The monster, even colossus of a dust devil nearly a third of a mile in diameter completely covered the slough. It must be nearly six hundred feet high, spinning in slow-motion in a counter-clockwise direction. There was a dazzling aurora of light overhead. It was completely silent ... completely unreal. Manfred almost fell as he staggered backward from the overwhelming sight that towered above him.

"OH MY GOD!!! OH MY GOD!!!" ... he screamed to himself as he placed both hands on the sides of his head.

He heard or thought he heard Albert yelling. He turned towards the sound. Albert had come out of a grove of trees from where the rolling hills met the municipal road with a roll of toilet paper in his hand some three hundred feet away screaming at the top of his lungs. He threw the roll of toilet paper towards Manfred's direction

"SHOOT! SHOOT! SHOOT THE BLOODY CAMERA!!!"

Manfred turned to look for the tripod with the camera, to no avail. The swirling monster of dust with the fantastically, colourful aurora overhead had collapsed back onto the ground leaving only cloudy entrails of dust hanging in the air over the great marshland. Manfred was standing like a small child with his hands only slightly raised, not knowing what to do with them. Through the thick wispy dust, the lone railcar that was the caboose, stood out like a serene sentinel on the marshlands, guarding a great secret. It was then that Manfred had noticed the ancient lantern on the back of the caboose. It was glowing with an orange fire for a few seconds before it exploded in a blinding light that seared its way back through the windows of the railcar. The light blasted through the windows so intensely that it lit up the dust from the now defunct giant dust devil and temporarily cast the surrounding landscape into shadow. Manfred was forced to wince as he turned away. The light was gone.

Manfred was trying to refocus his eyes.

He had been, in a matter of seconds, transformed into a complete believer. But something else was happening.

Albert was slowing down, staggering, and clutching his chest. Albert stopped in the middle of the municipal road, mouth and eyes wide open, and dropped head-first down onto the dusty road. Manfred started to run to Albert but he knew he was too late. Albert was dead. Manfred had lost the one man ... his uncle ... who was on the threshold of knowing what may have happened to the kids, those so many years ago. Cradling Albert in his arms, tears streaming down his cheeks, Manfred whimpered softly...

"Don't die Uncle ... please don't die ..."

Manfred never felt more alone than he did at this moment in his life.

The funeral, in the days that followed was a sombre affair. At the funeral, Eduard was worried about Manfred but was happy to see his older brother kicking off the depression, at least for now. Willie James and Mable Morley along with Evelyn and Rolf's sister and inseparable friends Cynthia with her husband, Charlie Hadquil, turned up in the town of Pilot Mound to attend the funeral. It was here where Manfred once again met Charlie...the leading mechanic, at that time, for the Western branch of Air Canada. Charlie was known as quite a jovial, somewhat stocky stature, all around and deadly serious builder, a top mechanic in automobiles, aircraft and boats and boat engines. Charlie was very intrigued by the description of what Manfred had seen on the day of Albert's death. Charlie and Cynthia were from Winnipeg. Manfred asked him if he would like to take a look at the site. Charlie thought it a wild goose chase.

Evelyn and Cynthia were each others' bridesmaids and had known each other and were the best of friends since their twenties. Charlie knew Manfred when Manfred was a young kid ... so they weren't complete strangers.

Manfred mentioned to Charlie about the phenomena of his teeth aching at the moment he threw the nickel into the air. Charlie immediately recognized this and the strange colour of lights Manfred observed overhead, as an electromagnetic phenomenon. He was also aware that no one had any back story of the caboose's origins.

"What the hell ..." Charlie thought.

This would be an interesting diversion. And so, Charlie's wealth of electro-mechanical theory was brought into play. Charlie went out with Manfred for a couple of hours on the dried up marshland while Manfred re-enacted the scenario associated with the event. Charlie told Manfred to dig down to the rails and find out exactly where they go... how far they went.

Manfred now, once again, had something to live for. The next day, Charlie and Cynthia headed back to Winnipeg, while Manfred visited Albert's house and wandered around it ... exploring it in more detail.

Manfred asked the family's permission to take Albert's books and notes, even his maps. The family had no use for them so, they ceded it all to Manfred. The rest of Albert's property was divided among Albert's family, including the tripod and camera. Manfred had to read up on these last two items before plunging his earnings into his own costly mechanisms. He transported all the books and maps of Albert's to his home in Larvyer.

Eduard and Anastasia headed back to Portage La Prairie. Manfred, for his part and for the next one and a half years prepared himself for the next event. He knew now it was real. As he studied Albert's peculiar maps, Manfred became an avid reader of all of Albert's geological and biological volumes. Manfred was slowly acquainting himself with Albert's knowledge of geologic time. He was slowly coming around to believing in something so impossible that it scared him. Even now he couldn't bring himself to quite believe in it but, the extreme possibility was dawning on him that all their children were still alive while lost in a warp in space-time.

Time travel!?!

It just didn't make any sense to him. He needed evidence and Manfred set out on a new life journey to collect it. He stayed in touch with Charlie. He did it sparingly so that he didn't say too much about the event. He wanted Charlie deeply involved and fully committed. This would require nothing short of solid, undeniable evidence. That is the way Charlie's world worked and Manfred always needed to remember that fact.

STRANGERS ON A DISTANT SHORE

It was just a raccoon. Benny nearly fell off his perch some fifty feet up in the spruce. The raccoon's charge was only to challenge him. It leapt to another branch and scurried away. Shock was setting in. Benny lay down on the branch he was on, shaking like a leaf.

"Damn!! That was close"... he thought.

He felt like he was going to pass out. He really felt weak. The others below started to call out his name. Georgi was on his way up with two spears mounted on his back. Benny looked up after some three minutes had passed and decided to investigate the structure further. Georgi was now only some twenty feet below him. He called out to Benny to see if he was alright. Benny responded affirmatively and continued his ascent to the platform. He crawled onto it and then ... stood up.

Georgi joined him about two minutes later. Georgi, ever the comic, looked at Benny and with a straight face...

"We heard a racoon scream ... or was that you?"

Without missing a beat, Benny retorted...

"He was wearing a mask and tried to hold up a squirrel. The squirrel got the jump on him."

Both boys continued the banter oblivious of the others anxiously waiting below at the base of the tree. Both boys had disappeared from view on the ground. The concern of those on the ground was tempered by the fact that both Georgi and Benny were safely on the platform. But something else was occurring. As Georgi turned slowly to look at the horizon, he noticed that someone was making their way through the grass towards the spruce tree they were in.

They were coming from the direction of their lofty camp in the distant oak. It had to be either Beverly or Devin. But why would they be attempting that alone? It was strange. Georgi pointed out the movement to the boys below ... coming at them ... through the grass. There was nothing on the platform. It was time to regroup with the boys below. The guys below may need to regroup. Georgi and Benny hastily retreated from the platform.

It was Devin. He was talking excitedly and pointing to an area about a mile beyond where they were now but, across the meandering stream bed, on the other side.

"...Guys! Guys! There's someone coming!"

When Benny and Georgi finally descended back onto the ground, Daniel turned to them...

"Devin and Beverly have sighted people moving in a group of about twelve or so. They all appear to be adults."

Who they were, no one had any idea. Now the platform was beginning to make sense.

"Maybe the platform is theirs'... you know ... to store their food and weapons!" Georgi spurted out.

"Or maybe it's a place to sleep or a lookout tower to watch game trails or something!" Benny added excitedly.

"If it was to store provisions" ... Jacob interceded ... " one or two hunters would have been left behind to guard it."

"Unless they moved on already" Devin enjoined.

It was obvious to the little troop of children that they now had to be aware of a new potential adversary in their midst. What worried Jacob was that if the little troop of kids could spot this platform then, the kids themselves could potentially be spotted in their home camp, up in their oak tree by this potential new menace.

Life was continually getting even more precarious, what with crocs, lions and now this added dimension of danger. With this hunting platform no more than three hundred feet away from the children's base camp high in the oak, the danger was imminent with this new threat moving into the territory.

"Guys. We're going to have to redo our camouflage ... make sure our lean-to camp up in our oak tree appears completely unrecognizable"... Jacob warned.

Their lofty camp high in the oak would first have to be studied from the ground to determine the extent of additional camouflaging to be done.

"We better get at it." Jacob stated.

The little troop of five boys made it back to their base camp and climbed high in the tree to try and observe the whereabouts of these strange people. They were a good mile away on the other side of the grasslands, heading towards the stream bed at a point nearly a mile upstream. Everyone could now see them. There was a good deal of consternation among the little crew of children about whether or not those strangers were kind and benevolent or dangerously malevolent. It was too much of a risk to take.

The extra camouflaging began in earnest. The youngest children stayed in the high altitude camp. Beverly stayed with them to keep an eye on the strangers as best she could.

Within twenty minutes, the strangers had entered the streambed. They had now crossed over into the meandering oasis of trees lining both sides of the narrow band of water. From there, they disappeared. Within that time, the boys had brought back plenty of branches to line the bottom of their sky high camp in the great oak. It was obvious that the strangers had stopped to set up some sort of camp in the distance. Beverly could make out tendrils of smoke some two and a half miles away. They had turned and gone the opposite direction from their oak tree. That was a relief.

It was time, Daniel thought, to do a little hunting. Mickey, Towzer and Skipper were running around high in their lean-to. They were always hungry, always whining. Their defecating and urinating were becoming an annoyance.

Georgi came up with the idea of building them a separate shelter lower in the tree. They would act as guard puppies alerting the children to any danger.

They broke into two little groups to hunt frogs, birds, even salamanders and snakes. Everything was fair game. Devin stayed with the little ones. Beverly, Georgi and Benny found a berry bush nearby. The berries looked and tasted like raspberries. They collected two pots full of them. Jacob and Daniel collected the small critters with the net that Henry had strapped to one of the knapsacks. It had a folding handle. They were collecting very close to the stream bed. They were on extreme alert for crocs in and around the grasses near the water.

They both decided to leave their bows to Georgi and Benny. They took along the two spears instead. The two spears were deadly enough. They couldn't collect and carry their cumbersome bows at the same time. If attacked, they needed these close-in weapons. The bows were long range weapons and couldn't be used accurately or fast enough for close in combat. They were taking an enormous risk.

Jacob and Daniel headed some three hundred feet upstream to hunt off the sandbar, ever wary of the potential danger of running into crocodiles. They both figured that where there were crocs, there was probably lots of small game. But that's not why the crocs were there. It was simply their basking site and they were very territorial. What bothered Jacob most was that neither he nor

Daniel knew anything about the behaviour of crocs. A few logs were sitting on the sandbar.

"Perhaps a turtle or two were around the logs"... Jacob thought ... "that might be interesting food."

Back at the shelter, Beverly, Georgi and Benny rapidly finished constructing a shelter for the puppies only ten feet under the main shelter that the kids occupied in their tree. It was small but efficient. The puppies had a new home platform. The little lean-to covered half the platform and was about four feet high. The puppies would have each other to keep company.

It was Beverly who discovered them first. A group of pronghorns, some fifteen or more, appeared some one hundred feet upstream on the other side, heading in the same direction as Jacob and Daniel. But neither boy had a bow.

Unknown to anyone, the crocs, submerged underwater, were stealthily following them as well.

After the puppy house was built, Beverly and Benny made a decision to each take a bow while leaving the remaining bow and spear with Georgi to watch over the three little ones [Vera, Gordon and Di-Di]. The two kids climbed down the oak and were away through the tall grasslands to join Jacob and Daniel.

Daniel wanted at least three of the older kids back up in the oak in case the tribal hunters were spotted. Then two of them could be sent to warn them. This did not happen. Instead, Beverly and Benny had prematurely left their oak camp merely to join them on the sandbar thinking that their bows might come in handy to down a possible pronghorn. That would be something.

Daniel and Jacob were already collecting small frogs by the stream. They had a net full of at least two dozen frogs. Both Jacob and Daniel decided that they were both pushing their luck in the croc's domain. It was time to back away ... carefully ... from the streams edge.

The rustle of tall grasses was loud.

Both boys spun around with spears pointing in the direction of the sound. They nearly passed out. The grasses broke open. Jacob and Daniel nearly peed themselves. It was Beverly and Benny, both with an arrow nestled upon their respective bow.

Beverly whispered loudly to the two boys...

"DOWN!!" Both boys crouched as Beverly and Benny stood up drawing their bows tight and released two arrows simultaneously. The pronghorns were running full speed across the water, onto the sandbar and back into the water to the side of the bank that the kids were on. As they came up, they were met with deadly intent as both arrows zipped by ... hitting none of the fleet footed antelopes. Jacob and Daniel kept low. They had already lost several arrows. Beverly and Benny quickly grabbed two more from their quivers and carefully aimed at the antelopes coming off the sandbar back into the water which slowed their momentum down somewhat. They would have been a little easier to hit but, the children were unskilled with no experience in how to lead a target. Benny's arrow buried itself deeply into the edge of the sandbar.

Beverly's arrow missed her intended target as well but with incredible luck struck another pronghorn antelope just getting up onto the sandbar. The missile pierced the antelope's thigh and pelvic region, crippling it. It fell onto the sandbar thrashing wildly. The rest of the pronghorns cleared the bar and were heading across to their side. They were trying desperately to avoid the bow shooters.

Daniel quickly raised his hand yelling at Beverly and Benny to cease their actions.

They now had to retrieve the arrow embedded in the sandbar and the pronghorn itself. Daniel handed the net over to Beverly while he and Jacob did something only a child or a seriously deranged adult would do. Despite the fact that the crocodiles were alerted by the splashing and blood from thrashing antelope and heading towards the sandbar from every direction, the two boys, nevertheless headed out into the water. The younger children instinctively knew how insanely crazy this was and were screaming at the two older boys to get out of the water. Jacob and Daniel were already half way out to the sandbar, knee deep in extremely dangerous water. No crocs in sight but, the toothy predators were coming in fast. A giant croc was keeping the other crocs out of the vicinity. This was his territory. Even the giant cats were very wary of him. The boys were now pushing hard as they waded up onto the point bar, both realising how stupid their daredevil antics really were. The odds were rapidly piling up against their survival.

As the boys pulled themselves up and launched their speared attack against the injured pronghorn, the massive reptile launched her attack from the other end of the sandbar directly behind them. Beverly and Benny were screaming their lungs out at the two older boys.

Devin stood up on the oak's platform straining to see what all the commotion was about from his lofty vantage point three hundred feet away.

The boys, Jacob and Daniel, turned simultaneously around to face the monster croc. For such a massive animal, it moved like greased lightning taking them by complete surprise. Both boys leapt to each side of the huge reptile as it threw its goliath body between them slamming its jaws shut on the antelope. Daniel hit the sandbar face first before he scrambled to his feet again, spitting sand out. Jacob thought that he saw something out of the corner of his eye as he too rolled across the sandbar. It was a blur of orange and black.

The huge jaguar was already on top of the crocodile. Daniel's spear was still imbedded in the antelope's rib cage. It was still thrashing about even after the monster croc had let go of it to face a threat of which it had not been prepared.

The other crocs avoided the point bar altogether. Jacob, in a running sprint had grabbed the antelope by a horn and dragged it off into the water. Daniel had quickly joined him by grabbing the other horn. Neither boy cared about any crocs in the water. Their hearts were racing as the hissing reptile and screaming, snarling, spitting jaguar were rolling over one another on the point bar.

The jaguar leapt off the massive crocodile as the great reptile slipped backward into the water hissing at the extremely powerful cat.

Jacob and Daniel just managed to pull themselves up out of the water just as Benny with arm outstretched, finger pointing towards the sandbar, dancing terrifyingly up and down screaming...

"IT'S COMING!!! IT'S COMING!!!"

The jaguar bolted across the sandbar launching itself half way across the water as it plunged in with a splash. In the next leap, the powerful cat was at the very bank of the stream bed just as the two boys whirled around with the injured antelope, pointing their spears directly at the huge feline. It was much smaller than the lions but far more agile, faster and a lot more ferocious. It was bigger and larger than any existing jaguar. It was absolutely fearless as it brushed both the boys' spears aside with lightning reflexes of its powerful forepaws knocking both to the ground. It was between them and upon their antelope in a split second. Then it was gone ... along with their pronghorn.

Jacob and Daniel were both terrifyingly relieved that they didn't have to fight the jaguar. Neither Beverly nor Benny could get off another arrow.

The battle for the antelope was too confusing ... too fast. That was one cat that they had to be even more wary of than the lions. Too many close encounters, too many death defying antics for one day. Everybody was exhausted and scared half to death.

Daniel, soaked and dripping wet and trembling uncontrollably, turned once more to look at the retrievable arrow still imbedded in the sandbar. It wasn't worth it. The little troop headed home.

Once the child hunters climbed back up into their oak home high in the tree tops and had time to relax, it was then that Daniel turned to Jacob...

"These spears are useless against a big cat like that."

Georgi interceded ... "It's your sloppy and untrained use of those weapons that make them inefficient, not the actual weapons themselves."

"Maybe we should make something akin to a Roman Warrior shield and headgear"... Devin blurted out.

"Would that even be possible? It sounds like a lot of work..." Beverly added.

Jacob raised his hand to stop the conversation.

"...How about dinner?"

"That sounds like a lot of work." ... Georgi shot back.

Everyone got it. Everyone burst out laughing.

"You could always trust Georgi to break the mood when things got a little too serious and downright silly" ... Daniel thought.

The frogs were big and fat. It meant a frog and a half each ... three frog legs. The rest had to be fed to the puppies to keep them alive. Everybody agreed.

That night, it was decided that everyone had to hunt the next day. For dinner tonight, it was raspberries, meat and crab-apples. At least their diet was getting a little more varied.

The original beef jerky was finished. All their food now, was what they got directly from their new environment. The embers of their fire glowed in the night as they all slept ... with Jacob and Benny sitting guard to keep one another awake. That didn't last long. Soon, with the crickets chirping, the frogs croaking, the sky lit up by star-light, like a million candles flickering in the vast aether darkness, the entire troop of children were fast asleep.

In the night, Di-Di woke up crying for her mother. Beverly quieted her and she went back to sleep.

PLOTTING TIME

Manfred sat in his room with Albert's literature and strange maps but ... no diary. The children took Albert's diary with them ... wherever they were ... he did not know. Albert's private notes and maps were more important to Manfred.

"Perhaps", he thought, "Albert had left some sorts of clues".

But to study his maps, Manfred needed some background in the kind of science that Albert, as an amateur, was very familiar with. Manfred began his studies. Then it struck him. Manfred's Aunt Lilith, in charge of Albert's estate might be persuaded to give Albert's home to him in exchange for rent. After all ... Lilith was Albert's sister and often took to cleaning house for Albert.

It would be no more expensive than renting out a hotel room.
When Manfred later proposed the idea to his aunt, Lilith's family objected strongly at first. But Lilith had a special place in her heart for Manfred. She liked her nephew very much and went against her family's wishes by granting Manfred complete living access to Albert's old dwelling. The family relented so long as Manfred was able to pay the agreed upon rent. Though the family proposed a higher rent than Manfred could pay, Lilith cut the fee in half. After all, the family could always sell the house at a later date.

Albert had willed it completely to her. It was decided that Manfred would have the house but only for three years. Lilith, from time to time, would look in on Manfred. The visits were short, sweet and an inconvenience to Manfred sometimes. But he liked her company ... sometimes looking forward to her visits as a break away from his troubling thoughts. He was careful not to mention too much of what he was doing lest Lilith's family should pull the plug on his research.

Manfred had moved everything back into Albert's house of antique clocks. There were hundreds of them. It was like a store, more than a home.

"How did Uncle Albert stand the racket in here?" Manfred thought.

"Then again ... it might really appeal to Charlie."

For a couple of months, Manfred poured over Albert's notes and books. The fall weather was closing in. Manfred had decided to take Charlie up on his recommendation about the caboose. Late next spring or early summer, he was going to commence digging out the caboose on one side when another idea struck him.

"Why not get a team of archaeologists together to do this? But what would they get out of this? Only one way to find out."

So Manfred phoned the local archaeology club from Morden. They discussed it politely. Dr. Isaak told Manfred that they were presently tied down with more pressing matters at various sites throughout the province. It sounded to Manfred as if he were about to get the brush-off. The head of the archaeological society in Morden suggested to Manfred a different route to take since it was more reminiscent of a police-like CSI crime scene around the caboose.

Dr. Isaak would send one of his top students to look at the site and set up a group of volunteers. The caboose was infamous enough to attract home grown law enforcement wannabees and amateur archaeologists. It was the best Dr. Isaak could come up with.

Manfred thought it was a great idea. The dig would begin in earnest next year. Now was the time to devote to studying his uncle's work. It was coming together slowly but ... it was coming together. Manfred got his second chance at life ... and he was happy for the first time in a long time.

It was a long winter with lots of snow. This, Manfred could not have predicted. It dashed all his hopes for years to come. The slough ... that infamous marshland ... filled with water in the summer of 1959. There was nothing Manfred could do. In the brutal winter of 1960, the site of the marsh was blanketed by an enormous blizzard.

He had bought a small camera to shoot still photography and sat freezing inside his truck when the event once again played out its strange dance. He tried to shoot through the truck's foggy windshield but to no avail. The whirlwind appeared as a massive blizzard circulating counter-clockwise around the frozen marshland. The aurora of lights could be seen overhead. He resigned himself to simply take it all in. It was beautiful and awe inspiring.

He was glad it had reappeared once again at precisely three o'clock sharp on 08 January.

"I'll figure you out yet you bastard" Manfred said quietly to himself.

For now ... he was pleased about the reality of the event. The next event would be scheduled for the summer of 1961. He would be prepared. But his hopes, year by year, were dashed. In 1960, Lilith had died and Manfred had to move out again, back to Larvyer. The slough simply did not drain. It was never bone dry.

By the eighth of January 1981, Albert's house was long gone. It had been sold and moved to Pilot Mound. Manfred had been living in Larvyer for all those years waiting for the marshlands to once again dry up. It simply didn't happen. The old homesteads on both sides of the slough had fallen badly into disrepair. Several of the barns had completely collapsed. Many of the wires from the telephone poles leading up to the farm houses were lying on the ground. The farms were now ghost farms.

It was late one evening when Manfred had driven his truck up to the farm house of Willie J. Morley ... his father. Willie J. had passed away a little while ago. Manfred's mother was still alive. Manfred's sister Evelyn had remarried and bore two children ... Fonzy and Loretta who became good friends with their cousins Samuel and Suzanne who were Eduard and Anastasia's offspring. Benny, Gordon and Daniel were Loretta and Fonzi's long lost siblings.

Though Eduard had inherited the farm of Willie Js. he and Anastasia had agreed to sell it. It was just a really spooky place. Eduard loved his father's farm and his childhood memories were embedded there but, so were the ever frightening memories of that event that almost got him and Albert as well. Once in a while he would visit Manfred. The two would often get into an argument that neither could win regarding that event. Eduard couldn't get Manfred to drop it and get on with his life.

One evening, Manfred found himself sitting in his truck outside Willie Js. old farmhouse in the courtyard. The engine was idling. The truck lights were on. Manfred was in complete retrospection. He peered out the front windshield of the vehicle down at the hood. For a long time, he didn't move. He slowly turned to look at the house. The screen door of the porch opened and closed with a constant banging as the windy gusts blew across the courtyard. Manfred sat ... quietly. As he stared at the porch, he thought he could see it light up. He could see his mother, Mable, busy in the kitchen walking back and forth with his older sister. His sister would be rolling the dough out. His mother would be sprinkling flour on it as the rolling pin traversed back and forth over the dough on the table. They would be talking ... then giggling.

Manfred looked up. He thought he could see Eduard's bedroom light. He could see himself crawling out the window with Eduard onto the top of the porch, then up onto the roof of the house. There, they would talk and watch the stars and count the meteors that crossed the heavens at tremendous velocities. They talked about Martians.

Manfred looked away and sighed deeply. Perhaps Eduard was right after all. Without Anastasia, Manfred wondered, would Eduard be sitting here in an idling truck an hour after sunset ... like he was now? He found it incredible that Gardenia, Di-Di and Devin had been gone for over twenty three years ... and he ... Manfred ... was still alive and kicking. A flood of anger swept over Manfred. This wasn't over. He shut off the engine. He turned out the truck lights. Manfred grabbed his flashlight and was out of his truck. He stood there beside the open door and slapped a mosquito that dared land on his face.

He hesitated a moment. Then he tromped up and into the porch. He stepped into the kitchen. The door behind him between the kitchen and porch hung off a single latch. His flashlight swept the small kitchen. He wanted to go upstairs to his parent's room and that of his brother and his. But he was afraid that he might fall through the stair boards while climbing up the narrow hallway. He thought he could see the steel galvanized tubs that they had once used for bathtubs and for collecting corn and potatoes from the garden. The tubs were sitting beside the old iron potbellied stove. Manfred could still see Eduard and himself in the warm soapsuds being scrubbed clean by their mother. They were excited to be going into the "big town" of Pilot Mound, to buy cotton candy, go to a movie and listen to a band play near the carousel.

The memory quickly faded as he swept the beam of the flashlight down the length of the kitchen. At the end of the kitchen, he could see his father, Willie J. sitting quietly, beside the little kitchen window, putting down his pipe, folding his hands on his lap and listening to the forlorn whistle of a steam engine in the distant darkness passing through the small hamlet of Larvyer.

Manfred was about to walk down the length of the kitchen but hesitated. Instead, he stepped into the dining room. He stopped at the entrance as if not wanting to disturb an ongoing festivity. He could see the long oak table and his father at the opposite end, head bowed, quietly uttering a Christian grace of thanks. It was Thanksgiving. He could see the turkey and all the trimmings, the plates of food being circulated around with mom and his sister going back and forth around the table making sure that everything was out before seating themselves once again ... the gentle glow of the candlelight, the laughter, the talk about the football game. It all faded into distant memory. The bright warm glow of that ancient candlelight winked out.

Manfred strode across the now desolate and dark room to the door where the ancient phone used to sit on the wall beside it. The door had long ago been boarded up. The dining room windows were broken. He stood there quietly. He didn't know why he was there.

He thought he could hear once again the forlorn whistle of a bygone steam engine. But it was just the wind whistling across the sharp edges of the broken glass of the dining room window.

Manfred was attempting to make a momentous decision for himself. His life was over. It was finished. He knew that now. The slough had defeated him. Then again, it struck him

"...Could it be, that after all these years that the slough of Morley Lake was really beckoning him to step through its wondrous doorway into another world? Could he and Albert, after all these years have missed the meaning of it all? But wait a minute!?!"

Manfred thought. "Didn't Albert actually go through that doorway? Had he not returned? Was Albert just too frightened to do it again? What if ..."

Manfred let out a scream of terror as something unworldly touched his shoulder. He had whirled around slamming his back against the wall to face whatever it was that touched him. It was Eduard.

"What's wrong with you man?!? I've been calling you"... Eduard said quietly.

"WHERE THE HELL DID YOU COME FROM??!" Manfred yelled back.

He was trying to take deep breaths to calm his rapidly beating heart.

"Mannie, I'm sorry. I was just in from Portage La Prairie to see you. Thought I'd take a trip out here. Then I saw some truck lights wink out. I didn't know it was you." Eduard stated to Manfred

"Why are you here?!?" Eduard continued.

"I had to take one last walk through here Ed. I've given up on this thing. I've been running away from it all my life ... I'm through running."

Eduard was glad to hear it. He put his hand upon Manfred's shoulder. Why don't we go back to town? Manfred walked side by side with his brother and took one last look around.

He knew he would never be back. He couldn't tell Eduard. As Manfred climbed into his truck and drove out through the courtyard, Eduard, climbing into his own car, glanced at the old house. He thought he could see Manfred and himself sitting on the roof of their old home. He turned around and thought he could see his entire family in their garden between the stocks of corn. He could see himself, Manfred and Evelyn chasing each other while his mother would call out to them to quit horsing around and pick the cobs of corn. He could see his mother's skirt blow gently in the breeze as she bent down to pick up the cobs that had missed the basket. Eduard cleared his memory and followed Manfred out of the courtyard.

FROM THE ICEFIELDS THEY COMETH

The next morning, the children woke up quite early. It was freezing. Something had changed. The blankets they were sleeping upon and the blankets that covered them just weren't enough to keep them warm. Why was it so cold? Through the tree top, the sky overhead appeared strangely as a greyish white overcast. The blue sky was gone. Georgi decided to get up and climb down. He didn't get far. As he peered out from their doll house, he was shocked at what he saw. Everything was covered with a layer of white. Parts of their oak were also covered. He turned to his brother who was now also wide awake.

"Jacob ... there's snow ... everywhere!!"

"Jesus!?! It's winter here."

Daniel rolled over and brought his head up. Georgi was right. In this strange land, winter was beginning. He also realized that they were going to need a lot more food just to stay warm. And that was going to be a problem. A blanket of snow is going to shield most small game.

Now vegetables and fruit were going to become somewhat of a rarity. They're going to have to hunt bigger game with all the inherited risks that that kind of life would entail.

"We have to become better hunters, better killers..." Daniel thought.

Today, they need to split up again. They needed to bring in more kindling to stay warm. It looked like a small dump of snow. Perhaps it would be gone by midday. Daniel and Jacob had read enough of Albert's diary to know that they simply hadn't been removed from their original homes on their farms to somewhere else in the world ... like Africa ... no ... no ... it was something else. Albert was alluding to the crazy notion of a move through time itself. But this was absurd. Still. How did they get here? And where was "here"?

Everything around them seemed very familiar. The older boys could accept that they were somehow transported to another place on their planet but ... not through to another time. If that were even remotely true, it would mean that they had never really left the farm. They were still there but, misplaced in another time. That would also mean that the space and time that they truly belonged to was somewhere back out there about a mile from where they first came to being here. That meant somewhere back out in the middle of the grasslands ... a place they weren't too keen to be again. It all seemed too stupid to believe in. Surely not...

It was then ... as Daniel was running this scenario through his mind that they were all awoken to a new reality that was thrust upon them before they had a chance to take in the changing weather pattern. There was a loud swooshing sound like an enormous beast breathing and then a familiar trumpeting from a group of animals.

Everyone looked at each other. They all knew by now to be extremely quiet ... excited yes ... but quiet until they had a chance to analyse this new scenario in such a dangerous land. Georgi crawled out of their doll house to get a better look. Below, all around their tree house, there was a large group of giant massive creatures slowly making their way past the grove of oak trees that they were in. By now, everyone was up. Everyone knew to be quiet. They could see the tops of the heads and backs of the massive giants. The elephantine-sized giants were covered with dense reddish brown fur. The older children sat in awe and were all aware of how their new situation was quickly reinforcing the extraordinary possibility that their small troupe were caught up in some sort of time travelling event.

The last of these animals disappeared off the planet some 4,000 years ago making their last stand in Northern Siberia. But in North America they had been gone some 10 - 12,800 years ago in the very early Holocene. Yet, here they were. The children were sitting in an oak tree in the very midst of these behemoths. Uncle Albert was right; they were truly moving through time and space thanks in large part to the mysterious Lake Morley. The conclusion was now inescapable. With that new knowledge, there was the chilling realization that they were truly on their own. There was no going home. They whispered among themselves that it was not a good idea to tell the little ones. It would be a long while before they would be able to break this news to them.

It was hard enough for the older ones to come to grips with the new found reality pertaining to their present situation.

The giants continued to move under them in a long slow procession. It was awe inspiring. Their giant well padded feet pushed the snow up ahead of their every step. They were the new denizens here in the grasslands. The children's realm was now imbedded in a herd of colossal mammoths. They were everywhere. They were loud as they trumpeted back and forth to each other.

Suddenly, they stopped in their tracks. They began to pull up the grasses under the light sprinkling of snow. They had now settled into a feeding mode. There were now some forty of these goliaths spread out for nearly two thirds of a mile.

In amongst these giants were some five calves. The entire herd of mammoths was composed of some three or four separate families that had united for some long migration to who knows where.

It was then that Devin and Beverly quickly stood up in a startle. Something ominous was happening at the other end, the rear of the herd. One of the mammoths was loudly trumpeting in a great deal of stress. It was surrounded by the visitors that they had seen only yesterday. Those visitors had been preparing an ambush all this time and now had just finished closing the trap. The visitors were running in and out from under the colossal creature at the rear of the herd, just before that mammoth's rear legs gave way and the animal collapsed onto its haunches. Then ... it keeled over ... raising its head and trunk only once more before collapsing inert in the snow. The butchering began. The visitors swarmed over the massive body. In the distance, they looked like ants on a large hairy victim. The children were mesmerized. In no time at all, they witnessed the massive furry coat slip off the animal's body. A huge red stained body contrasted itself on the white snow.

The dead colossus had been scalped of its coat. They watched as six of the visitors began rolling up the coat. The other mammoths now sensed that an extreme danger was in the rear of the herd. Some turned to look. The sight of one of their dead laying on the snow with its fur removed, panicked the herd. They started to move through the grove once again.

It was not safe here anymore. The children watched spellbound as the massive herd of elephantine creatures resumed their migration forward passing directly under them. But something more ominous was happening. The visitors were still behind the herd. They had caught up to the second mammoth.

Within five minutes, another mammoth had toppled over. The children could clearly see that the visitors were running in and out from behind the animal before toppling it over. It gave Daniel an idea. He huddled everybody together and a plan was hatched and it was dangerous. After retrieving a second huge coat from the mammoths, the visitors retreated, heading into the thicket of spruce trees. They were close ... very close. The little lean-to, filled with kindling, at the base of their oak tree might be seen. It wasn't.

The visitors were too focussed on their prize. They were also retreating ... heading back, as they neared the oasis of trees ... disappearing into them. They were now more that three thousand feet distant and still retreating, as the last one vanished into the forest of spruce trees.

"It was time" Daniel thought...to put their daring and very dangerous plan into operation.

The children waited. For the first time, the older children were going to abandon the little ones. Everybody was needed. The little ones were to watch for any signs of the visitors.
Vera and Di-Di were to stay put in their lean-to while Gordon was to shimmy down the tree, drop to the ground and run to warn the others if the visitors were spotted. The boys had tied a hemp rope to the last branch to allow easy access to the ground. The three little ones had used this many times.

Daniel, Jacob and Beverly carried the bows. Devin, Benny and Georgi carried the spears. They were to be absolutely quiet in executing their plan at all times. Jacob emphasized that this was absolutely crucial. Everybody was ready and confident and scared half to death. They waited. The giants lumbered past. It was nearly a half hour before the last three brushed by under their oak tree. What was unexpected was that the last ones were one adult and a calf. The calf was lagging behind and the children didn't know to which adult it belonged. It was a 50/50 chance. As the last two mammoths passed under them, the children launched their attack.

They were down quickly. Within four minutes all the children were standing at the base of their oak tree. Everyone knew what to do. The chase was on. The mammoths were now some three hundred feet away. The giants had ploughed several five foot wide paths through the tall snow covered grass. It made it easier for the children to follow but it also exposed them to extreme danger. They were in the vicinity and heading back towards the oak tree that served as an open-air lions den. They had to be quick. There was a pride of giant cats out there that were possibly cold, hungry and on the prowl. The children were running for their very lives.

Within a few minutes, they had passed the baby mammoth and were closing in rapidly on the first adult. Jacob and Beverly reached the mammoth first and took up their positions beside it ... keeping pace with the giant's strides. Daniel slowed his pace so that he was directly behind the colossus. All three bow hunters were positioned to protect the spear wielding children.

Georgi was the first to approach the one giant from behind and thrust his eight foot spear up between the mammoth's thighs with all the strength he could muster. Devin plunged his spear in next. The giant trumpeted loudly. Georgi thrust up into the giant again and again. Benny joined them both, thrusting his spear up under the mammoth. They continued for a few minutes. The giant trumpeted again and again but kept on moving.

They were now dangerously far away from the protection of their giant oak. They had probably gone some eight thousand feet. Still, the giant continued to stride. Then ... Georgi had a crazy idea. He thrust his spear into the giants left ankle. The mammoth raised its hind foot high, snapping the spear right out of Georgi's hands, sending him flying forward into the snow.

At that precise moment, the giant collapsed down on her left leg. But rather than sitting down on its haunches, it was toppling over. Georgi had only a second to react. As the giant collapsed he attempted to scramble out of the way but, the giant's back side narrowly clipped him and threw Georgi once again into the snow. Georgi's lower legs were caught under the giant's body.

The mammoth trumpeted yet again. Its trunk was swinging wildly. It was kicking with its right foot. The children were not skilled at this sort of thing. The stronger visitors were able to kill their two mammoths faster because of their superior skill and strength. The older children with their mouths wide open thought that Georgi had been killed. Beverly screamed. Jacob was the first there but Georgi had already extricated himself from the giant. He was limping but otherwise not the worst for wear.

Georgi narrowly escaped being crushed to death. He had gained a new found respect for the power of a mammoth. The children stood around the fatally injured giant. The herd kept moving. The last giant turned and stood. No one knew what was going to happen.

Then ... it charged. The children immediately ran from the killing site in all directions. It was a mock charge. The children stood where they were. Behind Beverly stood the baby mammoth. Everyone knew not to get between that one adult and the baby.

Another hour passed. The injured giant had bled out. Finally, the standing adult trumpeted and turned hoping the baby would follow. It didn't. The spear wielding children decided to poke the giant in the soft padding covering the hind feet. Jacob warned the kids not to stand directly behind the spear lest the giant drive it into them with a kick. After a few jabs, there was no response from the giant.

Now the gruesome part began in haste. Not a predator to be seen but the smell of blood from three dead giants was bound to bring every predator for miles around but so far, so good. The longer they were at the site the greater their chances of being discovered. They had to work fast. Time was against them.

But how do you skin a mammoth? They hatched a plan. The children climbed on top of the right side of the mammoth. Daniel grabbed a spear from one of the kids in exchange for his bow and quiver. Jacob did the same. The two oldest boys started, one at the back of the head and the other at the top of the tail. Beverly and Devin pulled the hide back as Daniel used the steel edged spear with the double toothed cutting edges. Benny and Georgi helped Jacob as they sliced into their end of the hide. Jacob and Daniel met together along the back of the animal. The hide was tough as the children began slicing the fascia away, but it was working.

Now ... how to get around the legs? Daniel had to slice around the throat and continue down the front of the foreleg. Jacob had to slice down the rear of the hind leg. It was the only way to cut through the fascia holding the skin onto the muscles. Next, Daniel had cut off about forty pounds of meat ... further cutting it into easy to carry ten pound folded sacks that were compressed and rolled tightly on one of their knapsacks.

The four small bags were used to tote the meat home since Uncle Albert had actually sewn on straps so that they would be able to carry them with no problem.

...Still no predators.

The children were still in the open and very vulnerable, becoming ever more aware of their dangerous situation. Gordon, Vera and Di-Di from their perch high in the oak tree and observing the bigger picture had no way of warning the others below of the coming extreme danger.

The giant lions had bounded out from the oasis of spruce trees along the stream bed. With pure, ferocious gluttony, they pounced with their half tonne frames of muscle and sinew upon the first dead mammoth that was toppled at the rear of the herd, ripping and tearing massive amounts of flesh from the carcass.

The three smaller children up in the oak did not know what to do. They didn't believe for an instant that the troop were going to outrun an entire pride of lions. They hoped that their older siblings would still get back in time before the lions had their fill. Beverly was the first to hear the cacophony of sound from the lion pride. She yelled her surprise for all to hear.

"OH ... MY ... GAWD!!!"

The children all looked up.

Georgi and Jacob looked at one another and started to run in the direction of the oak to protect the smaller children. If they split up now ... none of them would have a chance in hell of ever getting back alive. Daniel cried out for them to stop.

"WE DO IT TOGETHER!!!"

Jacob and Georgi knew that he was right. It took two of them to carry the half hide that they had retrieved. The older children had successfully removed the hide from the top side of the dead animal. They decided, realizing they had no time to figure out a plan of how to get at the other side of the mammoth hide, to abandon the bottom part all together. Half a mammoth was better

than no mammoth. They had rolled up their prize, tied the hide firmly with the hemp rope and were on their way back.
The baby mammoth was standing off to the side whimpering quietly. Beverly and the others felt responsible for its plight. None had the heart to kill it and skin it. It was sad but they had to leave it. The scent of its mother's fur instinctively drew the little creature to scurry up behind them. They tried to ignore it but it soon caught up and ran into their midst. The children stopped. No one knew what to do with this little calf. Then, unexpectedly, it toppled over on its side, after sniffing the rug then, slid about while rolling in the snow covered grass, pushing itself around in a circle with its hind legs, finally rolling over on its back side with its legs in the air, stopping only to move its tiny head around to see if anyone was looking.

It had found its mother again. It had also worked its magic into the hearts of the children. It only reinforced their tremendous guilt over what they had done just to survive. They let the little mammoth follow them. It had no fear. It trotted directly in step with them, sometimes rubbing its tiny trunk up against them. The kids started to laugh at its antics.

Daniel rolled his eyes ... "another mouth to feed".

The children had already given their new baby a nick name ... Woolly. The children were now within three hundred feet of home base. The little ones high in the oak couldn't believe what they were seeing. They were excited at the prospect of a new pet.

A group of fifteen grey dog-like animals were striding through the light covering of snow on the other side of the streambed at precisely the same spot where that spit of a sandbar lay.

They reached the streambed quietly and without even slowing their pace, splashed across the open water to the sandbar then, back into the water crossing to the children's side of the stream. As the last five snarling monsters splashed across, the first ten giant Dire wolves burst out from the grove, fanning out and surrounding the lion pride. The pack cautiously moved in on the pride. In short order, another half dozen Dire wolves joined the pack of killers as the last stragglers cut across the waters.

Without warning, the pack of twenty one Dires rushed the snarling half tonne cats. The cats were outnumbered nearly three to one but they held. Everything in this land was a giant far larger than its counterpart in the modern world from whence the children were abducted, it seemed. Everything seemed to be a modern day version ... on steroids. The battle was on between the giants.

The Dire wolves closed their circle around the lions snapping and slashing at their extremities'. The lions were on top of the mammoth carcass defending themselves as they leapt up in the air and around whenever they felt the wolves nipping them. The pack was beginning to overwhelm the lions. Two of the lions broke off. Then another lion scampered away. The remaining five were being bitten alive. It was too much.

Suddenly the battle royal between the two types of apex predators was over. All five remaining lions abandoned their prize. The wolves were also very careful in their strategy. A single blow from a lion could easily break the back of a Dire. The lions had their fill anyways. The wolves tore into the remains. They stripped the last remaining sinew from the mammoth bones. The lions strode by the second dead mammoth ... ignoring it.

The children were within two hundred feet of their oak. The lions came swiftly at them and cut off their approach to the safety of their oak tree. The children immediately gathered together; the children with the bows on the inside and the children with the spears on the outside. The lions quietly surrounded them. Beverly and Georgi began to cry but held their ground. The other boys felt sick to their stomachs. The fear was palpable and the lions knew it. But they were full and bored of the hunt for the day. Their bellies were practically dragging on the ground. One by one, the huge cats slinked off into the bushes to the nearby streambed to quench their thirst.

The Dires had already finished off the remains of the first dead mammoth. They were walking, no, running towards them!!! The lions had also noticed and immediately quickened their pace towards the stream bed. There was no way the children could stand up to the determined pack of killers bounding towards them. Even the baby mammoth had squeezed in amongst them seeking their protection. It too could sense the extreme danger.

The Dires raced each other to the second dead mammoth. The children were so relieved. Daniel had wet his pants and probably wasn't the only one.

"Can this get any worse??" Daniel called out.

The children turned and glared at him. Daniel just realised that nobody was laughing.

The children were no more than two hundred feet from the oak. The mammoth carcasses were attracting just about every mega-predator in the vicinity. Another such giant had heard the cacophony of sound emanating from the kill sites. This monster had the best olfactory apparatus of any of the mega predators. It could smell a meal from six miles.

This is why the visitors, had left their kill sites so rapidly. They didn't want to engage the mega predators. And this mega-predator was on its way towards all the commotion. No one could see it coming because this monster was following along the streambed and was not detected by the children or the other giant predators.

When this colossus burst onto the scene just four hundred feet ahead of the children, it took their breath away. A huge short-faced bear with front legs that looked like they were borrowed from a hyena roared into action. It was more than three times the size of a grizzly.

It turned quickly to snatch a glance at the Dire wolves covering the second dead mammoth. It turned its massive head sharply back around to look in the direction of the children. The colossus stopped and reared up to a staggering eleven feet high and sniffed the air for the aromatic scents wafting over the kill sites. It roared, lifting its massive paws fourteen feet high then, dropped to all fours.

Without a moments hesitation ... it charged. Its acceleration was slow but, it built up tremendous speed.

The baby mammoth trumpeted and urinated on the ground. Nobody could blame it.

Jacob yelled ... "Everyone!! Get back behind the baby!!"

The giant bear came straight at them. They could hear its heavy breathing as it ploughed up the snow in front of it.

Jacob called out "Wait ... wait ... wait ..."

The 3 bow carriers drew back their deadly weapons. The great bear started to change the course of its headlong plunge and passed the children at a staggering speed, running full out. It was close to within fifteen feet of them when it passed.

Daniel yelled and made a downward movement of the palm of his hand...

"PUT YOUR BOWS DOWN!!!"

The children did as commanded.

The huge goliath ignored them and the baby. It headed straight to the third dead mammoth ...Woolly's mother. At that, the children just watched and stared as the apex predator hurtled by them sending up a cloud of snow. Then, instinctively, everyone broke and ran, reaching the oak in minutes flat. Even Woolly was keeping pace. As the children launched themselves high in the tree and dragged up the mammoth coat, Woolly began trumpeting his distress.

The pups, Mickey, Towzer and Skipper were running and playing along the lower branches of their giant oak. The puppies came to the base of the branch which connected to the trunk of the tree as the little mammoth rose up and put its little forepaws on the bark of the tree while stretching its short tiny trunk up to touch and greet each small pup. The tiny baby had just made some new friends that it could better relate to.

Jacob suggested building a stairway up the tree to the dog shelter for the pups. This could be easily accomplished and would allow the pups access to the ground and back to their doghouse. They were now eight weeks old.

MANFRED'S LONG GOODBYE

By 1982, the weather pattern in southern Manitoba began to change. A much drier season made its approach. The winter of 1981 was a very dry, mild winter which afforded the surrounding locales with little precipitation. It was beginning to look like 1982 was going to be dry ... very dry.

There was now something happening which just might stagnate all of Manfred's plans to take the plunge through this magic portal. He was purchasing the equipment he needed as if going on a mountain climbing expedition. He was also going to take a high powered rifle ... a .3030 with him and plenty of ammo. This he accomplished in slapping together by March. He was dangerously low in funding. It was a last ditch effort to find out what happened to his family.

Then, it happened ... twenty years too late. It threatened to interfere with everything. The Historical Society in Morden had renewed their interest in the ancient caboose and had made provisions with the land owners to have it excavated and removed. Manfred once wanted this, but happening now would destroy his one and only last chance.

"What would they discover? Did any of them have the foggiest idea of what they were about to tamper with?" Manfred thought.

The Morden Society had established the time of the opening excavation as May 15th, seven weeks ahead of the scheduled event. Manfred had to ingratiate himself with the members of the Society and first introduced himself as the original land owner. He was willing to volunteer for the summer. The Society told Manfred that they would be happy to get all the help they could assemble. Manfred allowed himself to be taught by the Society how to properly excavate such rare artefacts.

Manfred chuckled at the thought that his childhood was spent in that so called rare artefact. Once this was settled ... Manfred got on the blower to Charlie Hadquil, the retired super-mechanic.

"Uncle Charlie? Mannie here."

After an exchange of pleasantries, Manfred explained what was happening out in Larvyer.

"I see..." Charlie began ... "so ... I wouldn't have to do anything but observe what was happening and to jump in when I think I could give some advice? I don't know. You would have a professional team there on site, so why would you really need me there Manfred?"

Manfred struggled to think of one. He was hoping that Charlie would be enthusiastic enough to jump right in. But that wasn't Charlie.

Manfred began to stammer ... "I ... I thought that ... maybe"

Charlie decided to throw his nephew a little slack.

"Alright, on one condition... Is there a golf course near the vicinity of Larvyer?"

Manfred was stunned but realised Charlie, an avid golfer, was not asking this in jest. He just wanted to have something to do other than stand around watching an ongoing excavation ... unless it got to be exciting.

"Yes"... Manfred answered back ... "about three of them."

With that done, Charlie asked Manfred to get in contact with him over this excavation IF they found something. He would then take the time out from his numerous hobbies and make the trip out to

Larvyer. Manfred signed off with Charlie. He seemed genuinely interested. It didn't hurt that Manfred also really liked Cynthia and Charlie a lot. After his internship with the Morden Society as a field assistant, Manfred felt a little bit more qualified. However ... they needed some back history and Manfred couldn't really provide much beyond his grandfather's and his late Uncle Albert's stories.

That said ... he was getting very excited about closing in on the truth. He would be the one, along with this team from Morden, who were actually going to find out what the hell was really going on.

He was still apprehensive about this excavation project. Should he warn them? Would they think he was an old fuddy-duddy who was going a bit senile? Better to keep quiet and let the stones fall where they might.

Something else bothered Manfred ... much closer to home. It was the young Connie Paladin ... Manfred's niece and Albert's grandniece. How much did she really know about this caboose and the events surrounding it?

Connie had joined the Morden Society at the tender age of eleven as a volunteer. She was fascinated by her great Uncle Albert's riveting stories about ancient worlds and that all of this was due to that "magic" caboose. Albert had taken her out to the marshland on several occasions but she had only met Devin and Di-Di. The others had not had the pleasure to meet with her before they vanished.

The time was soon upon them all. Summer was here.

It began in earnest on May 15th, 1982. The team from Morden had arrived and joined Manfred. After brief introductions with the hard hat supervisor on site from the land Company [who now owned Manfred's old farm], the moment had arrived for Manfred.

The Morden team got down to photographing the entire caboose from top to bottom, front to back, inside – out. Everyone was well aware of the stories about the missing children. The stories related by Connie to the Morden Society of her great uncle's explanation of their disappearance ... well ...those stories were received a little differently.

The Morden team had set up a camp on site just on the other side of the old dirt road leading up into Manfred's farm. The team had brought in a small trailer as a work and dinner station. They brought in a supply tent as well. The work commenced in earnest.

The excavation was deliberately slow, and careful. By the 29th of May, there was a small excavation pit around the caboose some four feet deep. The team had indeed discovered four pairs of steel wheels supporting the caboose. As the excavation crew worked its way down around the caboose, one of the worker's awls hit something metallic between the two sets of wheels on one side of the caboose. It was on rails.

As the excavation continued, it became apparent that the rails themselves were attached to a slightly rounded concave metallic cylinder directly under the railcar. The entire caboose was sitting upon some sort of cylinder.

It was time to break for lunch. The sky had become cloudy once again and the pall of gray began to completely cover the blue dome of the sky. It started to rain, effectively ending the day's excavation. For the next ten days it rained virtually nonstop, flooding the excavation and then filling up the slough with large isolated puddles of water. The dry slough was taking on the appearance of a small lake ... yet again. The weather was also unusually cold for this time of year. The Morden crew hoped it was just temporary. Nevertheless, the excavation was cancelled until the 9th of June. Mel told the Morden museum that he would watch over the site until they returned to commence excavating again. They agreed.

Manfred was hatching another plan. He decided to order in a metal-detector from the States. He had a strong hunch that there was something bigger in the slough. He wanted to know how far into the slough that the cylinder went.

The rails were mounted on top of it, almost as if they were designed to carry the railcar to another destination. He remembered the old stories about the railcar, over the last century, being in different places around the slough. The movement was imperceptible over a human lifetime but, if the stories were true ... It seemed absurd but, he had seen some crazy things out here and was more than willing to take the risk. What could he lose?

He was now in his small house in Pilot Mound. He had convinced Lilith to sell Albert's small house to him. During this time, Manfred spent his waking hours cutting and assembling over a hundred nine foot high metal rods and attaching to the top of each one orange surveyor's tape.

By the 9th of June, the Morden crew was checking out the conditions at the excavation site. They decided to hold off for four more days until the site had dried enough for them to climb back into it. By the 14th of June, the site had dried enough for the Morden crew to reopen their dig. It was freezing cold. The skies were still overcast. At first it began to rain again ...then it snowed. It snowed for the next five days.

As the cold winds whipped relentlessly across the prairies, the Morden society cancelled further excavations until more summer-like weather rolled in. The 20th saw the first blue skies overhead. By the 22nd, the snow had evaporated over the entire slough and the temperature was rising significantly. By the 24th everything had finally dried out completely. The 25th saw a renewed effort to get the caboose out of the excavation site. A small crane had been brought in to lift the railcar from the rails, but it was unable to do so. The decision was made to bring in a welder, but the museum society's only welder was unable to separate the wheels from the rails. There was no indication that they had been welded on.

The acetylene torch was unable to cut through. They called in a MiG-welder. Within another day, 26th of June, the welder had arrived. He set up his equipment and proceeded to separate the wheels from the rails ... to no avail. The welder was totally taken back by this unexpected discovery. He cut the torch, stood up, lifted his welder's visor and turned to the foreman raising both arms in a gesture of bewilderment before announcing that he personally didn't believe that this metal was actually steel. It was stronger with a considerably higher melting point than anything he had ever heard of.

The Morden crew was at a loss as to what to do. That's just where Manfred jumped in. His plan was about to hatch.

"Why not map out this anomaly first with metal stakes and surveyor tape while we're waiting for new cutting torches" ... he said in a nonchalant way.

"The entire day would not be a waste then, will it?".

It certainly appealed to the Morden crew's sense of scientific methodology. Part of the Morden crew was assigned to aid Manfred ...until needed back on the prime excavation target.

And so... it commenced.

Over the next ten days, the Morden crew was split into two groups. One group continued the on-site excavation. The other group of three did the staking with Manfred. The metal detector from the States had finally been shipped in. Melvin took an afternoon off to grab the device which was sitting in the mailroom in Morden. By the time he was back, half the day was over with. The survey crew was now studying the operation of this devise. It would help them to bury the survey stakes quicker. It was now the 30th of June. It was getting closer to the timing of the event. The Morden crew had known already of these stories and had viewed them as just ... stories ... much like hauntings ... a lot of fun and definitely for the tourists. It was good marketing. What else could you say about it?

By the 6th of July, half of Manfred's stakes had been placed into the ground, one on each side of the underground cylinder which in itself ... was huge. Its diameter was breathtaking. Now Manfred was beginning to taste that not so rare of symptoms ... fear ... not just of the unknown ... but a now palpable fear that they were being lead into something that was way over their heads.

They were about to begin to open a Pandora's box that could easily drown them all if it flooded into their tiny, vulnerable world. It had already become somewhat of a tourist attraction. There were now well over four hundred people that had set up outside around the slough. Manfred secretly wished he had never sold the farm. He could be selling garden vegetables and meats to the crowd for the barbeques that some of them had brought with them. But, there were more serious issue sat hand. The tourists were busy snapping photos unaware that they may be in immediate danger. The foreman had called for backup as people were beginning to duck under the barbed wire fence around the slough to get others to take their pictures.

It was the 6th of July. The morning was crisp and cool. But the forecasts of the weather bureau indicated high temperatures for the next two weeks in around 80 to 90 degrees fahrenheight scale. It was shaping up to becoming a hot summer. The cylinder upon which the railcar was sitting was a staggering ten feet in diameter.

The excavation was now taking on goliath proportions. The costs were running beyond the museum's financial capabilities. The stakes that Manfred's small crew were imbedding into the slough were spread ten feet apart, directly across from each other to get a sense of the diameter and some fifty feet from each other as they wound out from both ends of the caboose. What was even more spectacular was that the survey of the stakes on both sides over the underground cylinder were beginning to converge in on a circle.

The circle was within the depression of the Morley Lake marshland.

Charlie had finally arrived from Winnipeg.

Without being called, he had heard and read the stories from the Winnipeg Free Press and Winnipeg Tribune of the ongoing excavations and was highly intrigued by the new discoveries. Manfred was extremely relieved to see Charlie on site. After initial introductions, Charlie brought out a piece of paper on a clip board to calculate the exact size of the newly found cylinder. It measured nearly ten thousand feet in circumference ... three thousand feet in diameter. It matched the dimensions of the depression on the prairies between the two farms known as the Morley slough.

Charlie asked the crew if anyone had a radiation detector. Everyone in ear distance heard that ... and was chilled by it. One of the Morden crew spoke up, nervously...

"Why do we need that??"

Charlie looked down at the ground and then up at the tourists within earshot.

"I think this thing is going to pour out a lot of radioactive material. You've exposed it."

The "news" spread like wildfire. Within an hour, half of all the cars had left.

No one was staying around for that. Within another hour, only fifty cars were left and the people had them running and slowly pulled away to a safer location a thousand yards away, on the top of the prairie overlooking the slough. The foreman turned to Charlie as did the rest of the Morden crew and caught Charlie's wink and sly smile as he turned his gaze from the remaining cars on the prairie rim. The foreman breathed a sigh of relief and thanked Charlie. Everyone began to laugh. But he soon wiped the smiles from the faces of everyone present as he repeated...

"Can someone get me a radiation counter?"

The foreman stepped in ... "but I thought you said ..."

"That was to get the tourists to a safer place, away from here ... just in case." Charlie said...

"Now someone get me a goddamn radiation counter!!!"

The crew moved swiftly as one of them jumped into a vehicle and headed down to Larvyer to telephone Morden to tell them the news. They needed a Geiger-counter. The foreman for the company announced loudly that everyone was to exit the dig site. He notified his company that they may be in over their heads with this new revelation from Charlie.

Manfred, a bit shaken by this, strode over to Charlie...

"What are you doing Uncle Charlie?"

Charlie turned to Manfred and said that he too was like that safety foreman the company had sent out to oversee this excavation.

"When a new engine comes in to the airport in Winnipeg, I place only the most seasoned people on it."

Charlie leaned into Manfred...

"That's to insure that people don't have to die. Once we know all the specs and do our own testing ... people are free to fly our machines ... and not until then." Charlie placed his hand on Manfred's shoulder...

"We don't even know the specs to this machine...if that's what it truly is".

Manfred turned to look out across the slough. Charlie asked Manfred if he could stay for a couple days to witness this event.

Manfred welcomed Charlie to his modest home in Pilot Mound.

It was the 7th of July. Again ... the morning was crisp and cool. Manfred decided to take Charlie to Pilot Mound's Bed 'N Breakfast. There, one could have an excellent meal in a real kitchen. The wrap around balcony and the woodland surrounding the stately house might be what one would expect in a major tourist brochure. But it was homey. For the rest of the day, Charlie and Manfred talked about personal things.

The Morden Society Museum was still searching for a Geiger-counter. They realised that they needed to ship one in from Ottawa. The order was placed in. It would be at least ten days to get it out there by bus lines.

As morning drew open on the 8th July, Manfred and Charlie had breakfast together. After a couple rounds of coffee, they left the Bed 'N Breakfast for their vehicles. They came off the main highway between the Mound and Larvyer. Turning onto a gravel road Manfred and Charlie made their way down towards the depression known as Morley Lake. There were a group of cars, about thirty now that lined both sides of this gravel road. Both vehicles slowed down as they passed this mob of tourists.

The great slough opened up in front of them as they drove down to the junction between the gravelled road they were on, leading from the highway to the old municipal road that bordered one side of the marshland. The Morden crew was still on site but with only two members ... one was Connie Paladin. The other Morden member was a full time member from the Society.

The foreman was also stationed there and still had a cup of coffee in his hand. It was ten o'clock. Manfred had brought a video camera with him. He filmed the surrounding site with all the people who were there, including the tourists up near the top of the prairie.

This time he was ready. He was about to live the dream or nightmare. He was also cognizant of deep dark and fast moving

clouds moving in from the west. Out here on the prairies it was easier to forecast weather over a two week period.
The weather bureau didn't always score with 100% accuracy but ... they were usually close.

Manfred knew that only light temporary rain was forecast ... rain that wouldn't last for more than a few minutes over any specified region. They were just heavy dark clouds that were forecast to dump their moisture somewhere east of Manitoba.

Still ... it did concern him given the tight circumstances. By eleven o'clock, the entire western sky was black. Still...no lightning. That was something at least. It was finally happening. Melvin looked around him. He could see everyone doing their job.

Everything was quickly culminating into one grand act. Occasionally, Manfred could see people nervously glancing at their watches and then stealing a quick glance at him. He was becoming aware that he was slowly being looked upon as the center of attention. It didn't help that he had all that safari gear stacked inside the ten thousand foot ringed cylinder.

It was twelve o'clock ... high noon. The sun was beating down from a cloudless sky directly over top of the site. The other part of the western sky had turned a deep gray.

Eduard had arrived. He felt ... he had a premonition ... that Manfred was up to something. He had a bad feeling. Eduard's car came to a halt on the municipal road near the top of the prairie bowl. He was surprised to see journalists there from some of the small towns.

More tourists had arrived and were prematurely warned off by the company foreman.

Then, surprisingly, two cruiser cars from a couple of nearby towns arrived. The Company was getting worried about tourists on their property and possible trespassing and possible company liabilities in case of accidents. They phoned the police for backup for their

foreman on the site. The provincial police were there for crowd management only ... three male officers and one female officer.
They looked extremely relaxed. They were instructed to herd motorists up onto the top of the prairie overlooking the slough ... more because of congestion than really expecting anything dangerous to happen. Eduard introduced himself to the police. The two officers on the ridge of the prairie had set up road blocks to turn vehicles back around. Two more roadblocks were set up on the road leading up from the canyon from Larvyer and another at the entrance to what used to be Willie Js. old place. The cops radioed down to the other cruiser car with the male and female officer.

The male officer got out and located Manfred.

"...Says he's your brother."

Eduard was released and headed down. Some of the tourists turned around and left. Others simply reparked their cars and waited.

Manfred and Eduard walked alone near the site. Manfred laid it all out to Eduard. He was ready to take the plunge and find the kids. Eduard closed his eyes and arched his back before straightening up.

 "Mannie ... Mannie ... Mannie" Eduard said quietly as he shook his head.

"You really think this is going to happen?"

Before Manfred could respond, Eduard continued...

"I know I saw some pretty weird stuff decades ago ... once when I was ten and again when I was twenty but ... Manfred ... this is going a wee bit far don't you think ?"

Manfred looked at Eduard "... then why would you be worried?"

The comment caught Eduard off guard. Then it was Manfred's turn to be taken off guard as Eduard leaned in and wrapped both arms around his older brother.

"In case I don't see you again ... you have a great trip ... and I'll see you on the other side".

Both brothers embraced tightly ... "you remember me Eduard ..."

Embarrassed over this sudden emotion he realised that Eduard had believed in him all along. Manfred turned and strode to the remaining equipment and hauled it up. Eduard picked up the remainder. They both looked at each other and smiled...

"You're getting as crazy as I am Eduard."

"I'll be relieved to get this crazy over and done with Manfred. Then it's down to Larvyer for coffee ... agreed?"

Manfred agreed as the two brothers laughed.

By one o'clock the deep gray clouds passed over the site, quickly blotting out the sun and darkening everything. The temperature had dropped substantially. A chill fell around the site. The thick gray clouds were so heavily laden with moisture, that they barely cleared the ground with a ceiling height below five hundred feet. One could feel the moisture upon one's face. It was like a light sprinkle of rain. That's when the fog moved in. The conifers and oaks of Willie Js. farm were no longer visible. Visibility was crashing fast.

By twenty past, the dense fog had now rolled over the slough and like a great gray blanket, had covered the site. The cars on the top of the prairie were no longer visible. The site was no longer visible to them as well. Several vehicles started up and left the scene. The officers radioed to one another that it was getting dark and difficult to see ... one more thing Manfred hadn't counted on.

The male and female officers at ground zero broke out there thermoses and had coffee. The blue and red flashing lights of their cruisers were now barely noticeable in the deep gray fog.

The lit lanterns around the site were reminiscent of a scene from a graveyard. The dig broke off and everybody headed into their tents. The tents themselves with their lanterns were lit up like fire-domes in the middle of the dense darkening fog. People were sitting down and having lunch while they waited for the fog to break. The initial excitement as to what might happen was replaced by a morbid fear of being caught in the dark if it did happen.

It was two o'clock. The fog was deep and menacing. Manfred was getting concerned as the fog continued to deepen. He was having a coffee with Eduard.

"Might as well really enjoy this ... probably my very last coffee" Manfred uttered.

Eduard took a sip of his...

"I thought you packed a coffee pot and a bag of coffee with you??"

Manfred looked down quietly...

"Only if I don't survive the trip..."

There was a long silence as both silently sipped their coffees.

Eduard started ... fumbling for the right words...

"If you should ... you know... see the kids again..."

Manfred interdicted...

"I'll tell them that their uncle said hello and was wondering how you guys were doing ... not to give up the hope of coming back ...again."

Two cups of coffee later, Manfred looked at his watch and then jumped...

"Holy crap Eduard ... it's 2:56 ... I've almost missed this thing."

Manfred banged his coffee mug on the table and punched Eduard in the shoulder...

"Tell mom and Eve I'll be back with the kids!!"

All Eduard could do was stand slack jawed while watching Manfred burst out of the tent into the deep fog. Eduard strode to the tent door and watched Manfred's figure wander first one way, then the next as he was now having difficulty finding his way towards his safari gear. Eduard himself felt that even he would be having difficulty in this heavy soupy fog.

He watched Manfred in the dense ground cloud as Manfred deliberately strode in one direction straight for the marshland and his gear. Eduard looked at his watch. It was less than a minute to three o'clock. He slowly raised his head as if to peer through the opaque fog which had enveloped everything ... just to try and catch one last vision of Manfred ... in case ... just in case ...

The male and female officers were sitting, chatting in their cruiser quietly to one another. The male officer had his back to the slough, leaning against the inside of the driver's door while conversing with the female officer who was seated in the front passenger seat. Each were drinking their coffee from their thermos cups.

"I was checking on this Eduard Morley. Seems he was one of the prime suspects in the disappearance of those nine kids"... the male officer retorted.

"No shit!!" the other officer commented ... "I guess we find out now whether or not his story was bogus."

"Oh it's bogus alright"...Corporal Fred responded.

Officer Christine added...

"What, you don't believe in magic anymore Fred?? What happened ... someone tell you there's no Santa Claus?"

Fred smiled and looked at Christine...

"That'll be enough out of you young lady ..."

Christine sat back and with a deep sigh added...

"I wonder ..."

Fred perked up...

"Oh come on Christine ...you don't seriously think ..."

"What time is it Fred?"

As Fred shuffled some papers to look at his watch, Christine had dropped her cup on the front console spilling coffee everywhere.

"Aaahh!! Christine!!"

Fred caught the expression of complete surprise on his partner's face as she backed out the passenger door and stood bolt upright. In that brief moment, Fred caught a reflection of light that lit up the inside of their cruiser emanating from the mirror and reflected off the cruisers glass windows.

Fred snapped his head around. Coming from the dense fog were brightly lit sparkles of brilliant blue-white balls of energy lighting up everything for a mile around. A strange aurora of multi-hued light danced far above them. The fog seemed to be moving in a counter clockwise motion almost like a giant tornado.

Fred turned to his partner...

"CHRISTINE !!! GET IN HERE !!!"

Christine screamed back...

"FRED!!! GET OUT HERE!!! YOU'VE GOTTA SEE THIS!!!"

In that moment against his better judgement, Fred hurtled out the door of his cruiser. He slowly looked up. He could scarcely believe what he was seeing. There was no sound. The brilliantly bright aurora was reflecting its light for miles around.

As Fred's mouth dropped open he heard Christine quietly proclaim

"... believe in magic now Fred?"

Then ... in an instant ... it all blinked out ... plunging everything back into a gray darkness. But there was a strange amber light deep inside the fog in roughly the location of the caboose. It shone ever brighter before it too ignited in a brilliant flash that lit up the entire country side before it too blinked out.

There was no sound. No one moved. No one said anything except Fred as he whispered loudly to himself

"You don't see that everyday ..."

He turned to Christine, speechless. Christine lowered her gaze and looked straight at her partner...

"No, you don't Fred..."

Christine shifted her stare to look out across the slough...

"Not everyday" ... she whispered ..."Not ever."

Eduard dropped his coffee onto the ground. He didn't even notice. All he could think of was Manfred.

He started to yell...

"...MANNIE!!! MANNIE!!! MANFRED!!!"

At that moment he could barely see a half dozen other figures moving around in the fog. One came out of the dense fog nearly scaring him half to death. It was Connie...

"Where's Manfred?"

Eduard hesitated for a brief moment to answer Connie. In a flash of memory he could see himself and Manfred as little kids doing all sorts of crazy things on the farm but ... they were always together. Without taking his eyes off the dense rotating fog and brilliant aurora overhead he answered slowly, quietly...

"He's ... gone."

The aurora was so brilliant that those who stayed on the prairie rim were overwhelmed. The dense fog seemed to bounce the colourful light from the aurora over several square miles. It was later said that even towns within twenty miles of the site could see it.

Charlie was still holding his cup of coffee...

"Now THAT is more like it ... it must be electromagnetic!! ...maybe even ... dare I even imagine it ... a machine!! Now this is something I could sink my teeth into ... HAS ANYBODY SEEN MANFRED!?! Wait 'til Cynthia hears this."

In his excitement, as Charlie wandered forward looking straight up at the brilliant aurora, he tripped over one of his own tent pegs and landed on his face. He lifted his head up and struggled back up onto his feet...

"Well ... that coffee was getting cold anyways."

The buzz between the officers from the two cruisers was ecstatic to say the least with both sets of officers describing what they had just seen from their differing perspectives. No one could find anyone in the dense fog.

Charlie, a film documentary amateur professional didn't bother with filming the event thinking that the fog would hide everything. He was to regret that lack of foresight for the rest of his life.

The dense fog remained settled into the depression that was Morley Lake and its surrounding environs. The officers were helping everybody out of the area to safety.

They were taking descriptions from witnesses to the event. By six o'clock, only the officers of the two cruisers were ordered to stay there positions and report in with their findings when they were sure that no one else was left at the site. As the second cruiser started up to leave, Officer Christine pointed out Officer Fred's window seat and yelled to stop the cruiser. Christine thought she had seen a figure in the fog.

"Fog's just playing tricks on your eyes Christine."

"Yah, I thought I saw something move out there..."

Christine turned away from Fred and looked across the way...

"So what do we do about the truck belonging to Manfred Morley?"

"Let's leave it here for now Christine ... return tomorrow. It's off the side of the municipal road anyways...Ready to head out?"

Christine nodded and Fred took the cruiser slowly, quietly down the municipal road in the direction of Larvyer. In a few minutes ... the cop cruiser was gone. Only the taillights were visible through the tremendously deep fog.

All was quiet for a few moments. Then the frogs began croaking loudly. Crickets could be heard everywhere. All matter of night sounds were becoming audible. Then, a form, aimlessly stumbling around lost in the deep fog started shouting...

"HELLO!!! IS ANYBODY OUT THERE?!?

A MAMMOTH OF A PROBLEM

Georgi and Benny untied the mammoth skin and wrapped it inside-out around the tree trunk. With their spears, the defleshing of the hide had begun in earnest. Beverly was at the bottom of the tree tending to little Woolly. Jacob was collecting the fat as both boys continued to deflesh the hide.

Daniel and Beverly were discussing how to feed Woolly. It was decided to use the small pot to collect a handful of eggs, mix them with grass and water and hope for the best. Daniel decided to slice the grass into tiny pieces as best he could. Woolly might be able to get some grain out of it. A mixture was concocted for the little guy. He sniffed it out with his tiny trunk. The children decided to emulate his mother's trunk with their arms, dipping their fingers into the can and pretending to eat the mixture. Woolly caught on ... dipped his little trunk into the mixture and promptly spat it out.

Beverly turned to Daniel

 "What are we going to do?"

Daniel thought for a moment...

"Guess we wait until he's really hungry."

Devin interjected ... "That presents us with a wee bit of a problem doesn't it?"

Daniel and Beverly both turned to Devin

"What do you mean Devin?"

 Devin continued...

"A hungry baby that spits out its pabulum is going to be a very noisy one. He's going to start whimpering and then full out crying."

Daniel and Beverly both turned to look down at Woolly.

"Wait a minute! Why not a dozen eggs a day and mix it with strawberries to create a new and pleasant taste for this little guy? Beverly ... you collected strawberries along the streambed..."

Devin interjected again...

"Do you know how dangerous that is Daniel? Crocs! Jaguars! And who knows what else!"

Beverly immediately voiced...

"I'll do it!! But I'm going to need protection... two spear guys, two bow guys."

Daniel thought...

"That's a lot of protection but, Beverly's probably going to need it."

Finally he relented...

"O.K. but if that doesn't work, he's our next hide".

Devin had second thoughts

"Wait a minute. This isn't going to work. We can't find that many eggs every day. We need to feed ourselves. We can't feed an elephant and expect Gordon, Di-Di and Vera to go hungry along with our pups ... can we? This thing is going to take way too much of our time hunting just to feed it."

It didn't help Devin's cause one bit when Woolly put his tiny trunk into Devin's pocket.

It tickled and Devin bent over laughing...

"Cut it out"

...he wasn't in the mood to save the little mammoth's life ... try as he might.

Beverly had another idea.

"Tie his foot to a stake some three hundred feet away. Let him cry out. See if he can attract a herd of mammoths. Maybe another herd would readopt him?"

"More likely" ... Daniel retorted "... some predator or group of predators are going to find him first ... We would be sending him out to his death".

"Not really Daniel" ... Beverly said "... all the mega predators have eaten their fill ... they're stuffed to their gills ... they won't be hunting for quite a few days ... this buys the little guy some time doesn't it?"

Even Beverly didn't like the idea but, they couldn't afford to have a constantly crying baby right at the foot of their oak tree. It was just way too dangerous. Nobody wanted that. The younger children, Di-Di and Vera in particular, didn't want to see Woolly go. This wasn't going to be easy for any of them. It was going to be hard. The outcome could only end in tragedy ... either way. It was the least of the two evils.

The older kids tied some hemp rope to Woolly's leg but Benny recognized that it might cut into the little guy's foot, possibly crippling him in the long run. So a piece of flexible thin bark was tied to the wee guy's foot just inside the rope. It allowed them to tighten the rope so it wouldn't come off.

Daniel had been studying the different types of knots in Albert's survival guide. He found what he believed to be the appropriate one. With this knot, he lay out an extra piece of it nearly fifty feet long after tying it to Woolly's foot.

"What's that for?" Beverly asked.

"If the herd of big guys find him" ... Daniel said ... "then we pull on this, which in turn, according to Albert's diagrams, releases the rope around his foot."

Everyone gathered around Woolly one last time to say their goodbyes. Devin had an idea.

"Wait ... wait ... if he's going to be released into the care of another mammoth family, he's going to half to be acceptable to them by smell. My dad always warned me about cows and horses rejecting their babies because they didn't smell right. He would take a cloth and rub it on the mother ... then onto the baby."

He looked around at the quizzical faces surrounding him.

"Well it seemed to always work."

When the time had come, he smeared the fat from Woolly's mother on Woolly's coat of long furry hair. He would smell like a mammoth again. He would smell like a mammoth to the predators as well.

Jacob and Daniel took him out about three hundred feet from their oak tree. It was a long shot but they had to take it. The older children knew that it was highly unlikely that the herd would return for just one individual.

The rest of the children watched as the two older children pounded the stake into the ground with a rock. Within two hours, the stake had been driven nearly four feet into the ground. It was getting cold so the boys retreated as the young mammoth called out to them. It was very hard for them to turn their backs on the little creature like that. They walked back to their camp high in the oak trying not to turn around.

. . .

The fog had lifted over the slough as late as a quarter past ten on the hour the following morning. The police were there shortly before ten o'clock. There was no sign of Manfred's safari gear. There was no sign of Manfred's truck. What was far more startling ... there was no sign of the caboose. It was gone. Even the rail system upon which it sat was gone along with the cavernous cylinder that supposedly wound its way some ten thousand feet around the slough. It too had vanished.

Journalists for the Winnipeg Free Press and Tribune newspapers were also out all night interviewing people including the police. The journalists themselves witnessed the strange event but no one witnessed the vanishing act of any ten thousand foot cylinder. No one really knew for sure that there ever was one save for the cavern underground where no one was allowed access. The stories were all similar which added tremendously to their merit but not conclusively ... for the stories proved nothing more than people having an unusual experience together.

It did add immeasurably to the Morley legend though.

Officers Christina and Fred were brought in once again to investigate the site. The Morden crew were already there with them. Everyone of the Morden crew was standing around the site. One of the Morden crew members approached the two officers and was glad that they too had witnessed last night's event.

"We got something you should see officers ... maybe take a look at?"

The crew knew the two officers who visited the site from yesterday. The officers were already aware of the findings at the site.

"You guys successfully removed that old caboose I see ... you guys must have been here pretty early to do that ..."

To which the one Morden Society member said...

"We didn't."

At that remark, both officers stopped abruptly...

"Then who did?" Fred asked.

That's when the Morden society member opened her hands and shrugged

"No idea ... which is what we want to show you."

"I don't understand..." Christine said, taking the lead.

"Neither do we" was the response.

As the officers reached the edge of the site, Fred immediately noticed something.

"Where's that partially excavated cylinder?"

"If you look carefully officers you will witness a ten foot wide cavern going in both directions supposedly some ten thousand feet around the slough."

Christine spoke up "...Anyone been down there?"

"Not yet..." came the response.

The Morden society member turned to the officers and asked a rather blunt question...

"Are we over our heads on something here?"

Fred motioned Christina over to him for a somewhat muted private chat.

"As far as I can see this, Christina, we don't even have enough for the military to get involved. All we've got here is a hole in the ground".

Christina interjected "...But shouldn't we at least tell"...

Fred interrupted "Tell who what? You really want to stick your neck out on this as a career officer Christina?"

"Damn you Fred ...you...we both saw what happened."

"Yah Christina ... exactly what did we see? ... a weird electrical storm? ...A caboose that just might have been stolen last night? ... we only saw a few feet of that cylinder extending from both ends of that strange railcar ... we've got nothing left to prove that anything was really there except for that weird railcar ... at best ... a stolen antique."

"Besides Christina, we're here to serve and protect. Make sure nobody gets hurt out here. If there is some big hole in the ground ... like they say ... then that's the business of the Morden crew ... not us. If they find something that they need to call us in on ... different story. But until then Christine"...

Christina took a deep breath. She understood the punishing career hit that that might give to both officers. The other two officers made a similar decision not to speak too much of the event. These were the first signs that the event was going to be "officially" lost and later buried.

The Morden Museum Society turned to the officers and asked that they fill out a requisition form ... a witness list as well and for now look at this thing as simply a stolen antique railcar. They agreed to take the first initial steps to placing in a report. The officers responded that this had already been done.

"We need to have the site cordoned off for at least two weeks due to the possibility of an unknown radiation leak"... a concerned Morden member voiced.

"Is that really necessary?" Christine asked.

"Just a safety precaution until we get a radiation counter"... was the response.

That said, the site was on its way to lockdown mode for at least two weeks. The signs were posted later that day.

What the Morden Museum Society did not know escalated the spookiness of the on goings. The crew that was hired to lift the caboose from the site and place it onto a flat-bed trailer, had returned at five o'clock in the morning to attempt a lift with a larger more powerful crane. It took them only forty-five minutes to finish the lift. They were somewhat surprised at how easy it was. The railcar simply detached with no effort.

The crane operator figured that his small crane couldn't get the job done. He was careful of the fact that the welder on the site some time ago couldn't separate the iron wheels from the rails. The crane operator had brought in special hydraulics placed at the juncture of the railcar undercarriage that supported the wheels on the rail. The railcar lifted easily.

Once on the flatbed trailer, the railcar was hauled slowly down to the little hamlet of Larvyer. Once there, the crane and flatbed operators lifted the caboose onto the CPR line.

They would then have a locomotive take the railcar to Morden where the crew could then place it once more onto a flatbed and take it into the town. The CPR station was informed ahead of time by the lift operators who considered this part of the excavation their expertise.

It was considered, after they wrote up the contract with the museum, a little cheaper to send it by rail and then lift it again once it arrived at its destination ... the town of Morden.

But it was the station agent's son who placed the note on his father's desk. The son then left for the town of Winkler. There was an open window and a fresh breeze had swept the note onto the floor beside the desk. The caboose was never entered into the manifest schedule of the station agent's book.

Later that day, the Morden Museum Society was contacted by the removal crew. But it wasn't 'til half past eleven that morning that the museum was aware of the preparations or the whereabouts of their railcar. The crane and flatbed boys had another job to do and decided to contact the museum much later during the day when the locomotive delivered the caboose to the large hamlet of Morden. The Morden Museum still wanted to know what it was that was actually under the slough ... if anything.

. . .

The mammoth rug was laid up on their platform high in the oak. It would require another hide to throw over top of them. That's when Devin had the idea of heading out to Woolly's mother again. There's no way that the giant short-faced bear could eat even five percent ... let alone ten percent of a fully grown mammoth. The three mammoth carcasses still had the majority of their meat still attached to their dead bones. The carcasses were however, attracting many scavengers ... foxes, feral dogs and vultures among them. Most of the meat would probably be removed over the next few days. As each mammoth carcass is greatly reduced in size ... as Devin related to the others, then ... it might just be possible to get at the hide laying underneath those behemoths. All the children around nodded their approval.

"We still need to protect Woolly from those other predators ... those feral dogs ... they might see him as easy prey"... Beverly related to the others.

Daniel then stated...

"We can do that but, not if those big stone cold killers return over the next few days. I don't want anyone here to face them over a baby mammoth."

"It's way too dangerous"... Jacob added.

Everyone sadly nodded or looked down. Vera and Di-Di were playing with Mickey and Skipper. The pups distracted the little girls from the harsh reality below them.

In the days that followed, the children built a little climbing stairs for the puppies. They were beginning to become a little more independent. The children had no concept of how to train them. They used the tree sap to imbed small branches into the tree trunk.

On the first night, the baby mammoth called out incessantly. It was hungry and alone. Eventually tired, Woolly collapsed onto his side and rolled into the light snow covered grass. He was quiet now and out of sight. At least he didn't call out at night ... unsettling the children and attracting a passing predator. By the third day, Woolly was very hungry and showing signs of malnourishment. Once again, Daniel and Georgi put together a small supplement of grass, water and bird's eggs stirred together and offered it to the little mammoth but to no avail.

As they returned, the other children were shouting. Daniel and Georgi's attention were immediately riveted to the other side of the streambed about a hundred yards out. Another family of mammoths was passing by their site. They took no notice of Woolly.

Sadly, the inevitable was surely unfolding. Woolly was going to die of starvation or be killed by some predator. It was only a matter of time.

That night, Woolly started to call out. Jacob and Benny woke up. The two boys peered round their lean-to. Benny was the first to see in the pitch black, large shadows approaching the baby mammoth stealthily. Once on top of the baby's position, Woolly squealed out. Then silence. The boys looked at each other. Now came the gut wrenching sound of wet meat being chewed. Both Jacob and Benny began to cry a little while trying to conceal their emotions from one another. They didn't want to wake everybody else up and start a cry fest. It was too dangerous. Jacob only hoped that their little mammoth didn't suffer much. He quietly said goodbye, wiped his eyes and tried to go back to sleep. Benny was doing no better. Beverly had woken and overheard the commotion. Tears were streaming down her face. How to tell the others? That was going to be hard.

Morning came. Everyone was hungry. A light dusting of snow had fallen on the top of the roof of their lean-to. Jacob thought it wise to get down from their tree top shelter and investigate just what type of predators took Woolly last night. It was sad but important to do.

He had to find out exactly what was prowling around at night while the children slept. As he descended, Jacob quietly called to Benny. The two set out on foot, each carrying a bow and spear. When they got to the site where they roped one of Woolly's feet, the stake was lying about twenty feet from where it had been placed into the soil.

Around the site were lots of animal tracks. The tracks were round and nearly a foot in diameter. They were not predators. They were mammoths. Several of the prints accidentally over stepped on the fifty foot rope that was going to be used as a release.

Some mammoth had stepped on it while little Woolly was struggling to break free. The rope had a release from the stake and around Woolly's foot. Even the bark was there in the snow. It had worked. What they thought were predators chewing on wet meat was in reality ... little Woolly having his first suckle from a female mammoth that had adopted him. It was hard to say. Little Woolly was on his way to becoming a giant mammoth like his father before him.

Benny wondered if this future goliath would remember his fleeting human contact and those of the puppies.

Benny and Jacob looked at one another and began to smile ... time to bring back the good news. When they had returned, Beverly had already told everyone what happened to Woolly last night. It was a very unhappy little crew with half of them crying. Benny and Jacob's expressions changed the sombre mood. They related to the little crew what they had found. Little Woolly was safe once again in the bosom of another family. Vera, through her tears, asked if they would ever get to see him again. This was highly unlikely but Jacob not wanting to spoil the moment uttered a lie...

"...Perhaps."

WHERE TO FROM HERE

The small bell of the restaurant door at Barclay's Hotel rang as a group of excited tourists came in for breakfast. Other tourists had taken out rooms in the Barklay that night and had already animated the dining area in the restaurant with the recounting of what they had seen last night. The door chime rang again as a couple of members from the Morden Society stepped inside. They were going to catch breakfast before heading out to the site on Morley Lake.

In the corner, at one end of the restaurant, sat a dishevelled character minding to himself as they would say. Tall, gaunt and young looking for his age, Manfred was trying to rethink where to go from here. Right now, two eggs, bacon, toast, jam and coffee were all that occupied his mind. Manfred had found none of his gear that he had hoped would have been with him on his lone voyage to wherever his kids were. It was his last hurray and he didn't make it. Yet he now knew he wasn't alone.

He and Albert would no longer be thought of as eccentric anymore. He was part of an ongoing, unfolding legend. His family would hardly be forgotten now. They will live on as part of that illustrious folklore. It was all good.

. . .

A more serious matter was at hand for the lost children of the Clockwork Strange and they had to act quickly. The vultures were picking the remains of the mammoths very close to what remained of the hides. The vultures themselves were quite dangerous animals and would put up a fight if disturbed. But it had to be done. It would take all of them. Beverly, Daniel and Jacob grabbed their bows. Devin, Georgi and Benny grabbed the spears. They would tackle the carcass of the dead mammoth closest to them. At the foot of the oak, they collected their courage and headed out to the first carcass.

The cacophony of big vultures could be heard across the grasslands. Their six to seven foot wingspans were impressive. They were very aggressive and weren't afraid to tear a chunk of meat out of a living animal or each other. All manner of vultures had arrived ... most with smaller wingspans. There must have been several dozen of these terrifying birds on the carcass of the nearest mammoth. More were descending on the other dead mammoth ... Woolly's mother. The dire wolves had already stripped the first carcass clean and shredded the fur coat that that mammoth was lying upon.

The six older kids fanned out in a straight line while slowly approaching the kill site. The three bow carrying children each carried a long branch. The other three children carried the razor sharp spears. The children looked nervously around them for any telltale signs of any giant predators. It was now or never. Together, they charged the melee of birds.

The children had to be very careful that they themselves didn't get surrounded by all the feathered terrors. If any giant predators turned up, they would have to deal with them as a separate issue. For now ... these scary feathered and bloodthirsty killers required their full and undivided attention.

Benny and Daniel both remembered a close call they had back in their own world in a farmyard full of terrifying turkeys. As dangerous as those were, these vultures with their hooked beaks for tearing flesh were far more so. They dare not fall. To do so was to invite retribution on a nasty scale.

As the kids yelled and screamed in their attack upon these dangerous birds, the vultures themselves startled at first... rose in a tumultuous cloud of flapping wings ... dropping back behind and surrounding the children to assess these new competitors. Slowly, the vultures began to tighten their circle around the children, growing moment by moment more confident in their numbers. It was dawning on them that they could take these new competitors, and began to regroup to launch a retaliatory attack to reclaim their kill site.

Hunger was the driving force for the birds.

The birds had cleaned the carcass virtually down to the hide on the other side. They had not destroyed the hide as yet. The hide had to be retrieved now ... before it was scavenged by these birds. The children were attempting to strip the hide off the backbone vertebrae of the colossus and tearing at it from between the open ribs. The hide came off easily without much effort. They quickly cut the hide away from the fore and hind limbs. These, the birds had shredded.

Many of the birds had flown to the next carcass and were beginning the melee all over again. The children scurried back to the relative safety of the oak tree. They wrapped the hide around the trunk of the oak and tied it there with hemp rope, quickly defleshing the hide while waiting for the vultures to finish off the last dead mammoth. No other signs of danger confronted the troupe.

The hide was laid out to dry. Now it was down the tree for another hide. The lightly falling snow heralded change in the season making it imperative to acquire the resources to maintain warmth in this strange new environment.

Warmth meant further survival. Winter meant taking greater risks. Their growing experiences in this new world were teaching them just that. By staying alert and learning about the great dangers surrounding them, their survival abilities were increasing incrementally. Unfortunately, so were those of the predators.

Once down at the base of the oak, the children instinctively knew that it would be a high risk endeavour to try to reach Woolly's mother and retrieve her hide. It was well within the domain of the cats. There would be too many to defend against and they weren't trained to all concentrate on a single animal for maximal takedown effect. They would be firing wildly if it came to that.

The little band of children found themselves once again on a trek that would probably plunge the whole lot into a life and death scenario once again. They were beginning to get used to it. It was to be a twelve hundred foot trek out to that fallen third mammoth and another twelve hundred foot trek back. It was getting difficult to find fresh fruit and veggies with the covering of snow. Their source of obtaining quick energy was gone.

For now, the children had to concentrate on staying warm. The hide of this last mammoth had to be used for clothing.

The older children at the base of the oak were psyching themselves up for the final onslaught on that last mammoth. It was cold ... the vapour from their breath dissipating into the crisp air around them. It was still early morning. They were stomping their feet up and down. Some of the kids were still in running shoes. The fire in the lean-to kept the three small children warm at least. The older children were of one mind that the three smaller children were safe.

It was time. Jacob and Devin led the attack. The six were on their way to a showdown with these deadly birds. This time, the birds were not about to give up without a fight. It was the last carcass. The children were in a swift jaunt and picking up speed. It kept them warm as they headed out to the danger zone. They were now five hundred feet from their base camp high in the oak tree. Seven hundred feet to go. The children slowed their pace as they got to within sight of the carcass. They stopped dead and crouched down as they surveyed the landscape around them. They were now well within the territory of the giant lions. It was now or never. The little troupe of children was once again on their way. Everyone felt the urgency. It was unusual that the ruckus coming from the piles of vultures on the carcass had not yet attracted any mega-predators. As the children neared within two hundred feet of the melee, a strange new creature made its appearance.

There were six of these monsters. They were coming in from six hundred feet away and were totally undetected by the children. They were swift and silent. They were directly behind the children, and then a shadow over top of them.

The children gasped and froze as monster birds with twelve foot wingspans and enormous beaks landed in front of them and around the carcass. They were huge as they strutted in on the melee of fifty other vultures. The other vultures fighting over the carcasses were terrifying enough but these new giants were a force to be reckoned with. The other vultures immediately parted way for these new intruders. No one was going to mess with these monsters. The children realized they had to do something.

They decided to move in slowly. Devin, Daniel and Beverly carried the bows. Jacob, Georgi and Benny carried the spears. They were on the outside. They approached the fifty odd vultures. The smaller vultures with four foot wingspans parted quickly. The bigger vultures with seven foot wingspans stood their ground forming a ring around the kill-site. They only grudgingly gave ground when the little troupe of children were on top of them. Then the eagle sized vultures closed ranks as the children moved in. The giants with their twelve foot wingspans ignored them.

The children rushed the giants ... shouting and stabbing at them. This only annoyed these monster avian heavy weights. Two of them charged as the children quickly backed up stabbing their spears in the air at these giants. The two giants rejoined the other 4 and went back to ripping and tearing huge chunks from their dinner. Daniel was pissed.

"Alright, enough!!!

The first arrow sliced through one of the giant birds. It let out a hellish screech ... fell forward gaping and fluttering one six foot wing. Another giant caught an arrow in its neck. It too was finished. The other four giants stopped to notice. A third arrow drove through the breast of another giant which was left fluttering on the mammoth carcass.

The children moved in and climbed atop the gargantuan elephant. The three giant vultures jumped off. The children quickly went to work removing the hide. It was messy. Their clothes, hands, faces and shoes were soaked in blood but, they did successfully remove the hide. It was at that point that the ring of some fifty vultures moved in for the kill.

What they lacked in size they more than made up in numbers and they were just as nasty as the three remaining giants. The birds closed in from all sides. They were now leaping up at these new intruders and attempting to thrust their bald heads forward to snatch at the children. If they could reach one child, they could severely wound that child and easily pull him down. There were now many vultures leaping at them simultaneously.

From a distance, it looked like a ball of flapping wings, feathers and spear points thrusting out of the feathery ball of killers. Jacob screamed for everyone to back off the carcass and fast. The children couldn't hold up much longer. They were being overwhelmed. They started to fold as they backed off the carcass.

Daniel was the first to stumble, then Georgi. One of the giant twelve foot wingspan monsters was nearly on top of Georgi. The giant had seen him fall not more than six feet in front of it. The opportunity had now presented itself.

It was immediately upon him thrusting its enormous beak in and out between Georgi's legs attempting to take a really big chunk out of him.

Georgi, sitting upright on the ground, desperately thrashed his feet at the monster bird while quickly backing up. The avian monster kept moving forward thrusting its razor sharp beak at him as Georgi slashed back and forth with his spear all the while screaming for somebody ... anybody to shoot it. An arrow silenced the bird as it dropped into a fluttering heap of feathers. The children immediately surrounded Georgi to protect him.

Instead...the vultures immediately turned their attention to the dead mammoth. They now ignored the very frightened children.

Today ... the children had gained a new found respect for these feathered demons. Now came the trek back to their oak tree. A new twelve hundred foot dash was becoming imminent. They were still out here in the middle of nowhere. They needed to get out of there ...and fast.

. . .

In Barclay's restaurant, Manfred finished his first cup of coffee. Coffee never tasted so good. As he sat there at the table Manfred decided when he finished breakfast, he would go home and pour over Albert's notes. But what was the point now? Everything was gone. What more could he learn that would change anything? A few people at the restaurant from the Morden Society recognized Manfred. There was a flurry of activity and Connie went over to say hello.

"Mannie ... we thought you were gone ... I mean ... Eduard and I..."

Manfred interdicted...

"You thought I disappeared within that monster fog-like whirlwind

...that it had taken me with it when it disappeared"... Manfred threw his arm into the air ... "to ... who knows where?!?"

"Mannie" ... Connie said softly ... "everyone was worried about you."

Manfred looked at Connie ... "Enough to leave me out there?"

Connie looked Manfred sternly in the face ... "You know that's not true. We couldn't find anyone out there in that pea soup thick fog. We were yelling for an hour ..."

"Connie ... I'm just feeling sorry for myself right now. I didn't mean what I said." And with that, Manfred waved it aside.

"So what happened out there? Where did you disappear to?"

"Well ... Connie ... I couldn't see my own bloody hand in front of my face. I thought I was heading towards my gear, down from the caboose but, in reality, I was just following the barbed wire fence posts. I was never really inside that huge rotating funnel. I was just on the outer edge. I thought I was inside of it. So ... here I am ... and now ... there's no going back ... is there?!?"

"Why don't you bring your coffee over to our table?" Connie insisted.

But Manfred never did. He finished his breakfast and quietly left the Barclay restaurant. The bell to the entrance door rang out as more customers filed in and Manfred left. Putting his hands into his pockets once outside, Manfred was at a loss as to what to do. He stood outside the restaurant entrance for about a minute trying to collect his thoughts. He should phone Eduard ... tell him everything's alright...Time to get back to Pilot Mound. Manfred slowly strode across Main Street to his truck. He hesitated for a few moments then, slowly pulled his vehicle onto the main road and drove out of town ... passing the grain elevators of Larvyer where two groups of boxcars sat on siding tracks.

As Manfred's truck disappeared up the hill towards the top of the prairie overlooking the town, he adjusted the rear view mirror. In the distance about a half mile up the escarpment from the town, Manfred's vehicle screeched to a stop. It sat there in the distance ... not moving. Manfred was just staring at the image in the rear view mirror of the town below ... in particular at one of the group of boxcars. On the second track along side one of these groups of boxcars was a strange looking caboose with an ancient lantern hanging on its rear door.

IT AIN'T OVER 'TIL IT'S OVER

The children were cold, miserable and hungry. Jacob motioned to Beverly to grab the remains of the three massive vultures. As a safety measure, Beverly sliced off the heads of these dangerous birds. Georgi grabbed the second bird, Devin grabbed the third.

Now came the quick shuffle back to their base camp. It went without incident until the half way mark at two hundred metres or some six hundred feet away from the children's base camp high up in the oak.

Benny was the first to notice and pointed the anomaly out to everyone. Everyone gasped.

Beverly elicited an "Oh my god !?!" From six hundred feet away, sitting at the base of their oak was the jaguar ... quietly watching the three smaller children up in the lean-to.

The massive cat was on the hunt and very determined to snatch three quick meals in easy succession. The young child hunters knew they had no chance of ever reaching Gordon, Vera or Di-Di in time. Up in the lean-to, the three smaller children had no weapons with which to defend themselves.

Devin and Georgi could not see how it would be possible to save any of the three smaller children. The three fastest running children rushing towards the oak suddenly stopped short. The other children running up behind Beverly, Daniel and Jacob also jerked to a stop and froze. They didn't dare move.

A female lioness stretched out in the long snow covered grass had already targeted the jaguar and was within forty feet of the rosette-spotted feline. In its haste to grab an early meal, the jaguar forgot its own vulnerability.

The lioness's muscles tightened and then exploded forth in a cloud of snow closing the gap to the jaguar within ten feet, before the jaguar even realized what had just happened. The smaller feline turned towards its attacker.

The lioness was within ten feet of the oak, when the rosette-spotted huntress threw herself on her side to prevent the lioness from breaking her back. The jaguar had no time to run. The lioness was on top of it and not too surprisingly so were another lioness and a couple of massive males. Snow was flying everywhere. All five screaming, shrieking cats were fighting in what looked like a white fog of snow that they had inadvertently thrown up.

It was another, somewhat unknown smaller pride of four giant lions. One would have thought that the fight would be over within seconds, but the pride of four couldn't get a grip on the jaguar. It wasn't due to inexperience but due to the sheer speed, honed instinct and all out ferocity of the smaller rosette-spotted cat.

The pride had surrounded it but were leaping into the air away from their intended victim. All four pride members backed away from the jaguar while maintaining their ground. They had the jaguar completely trapped, leaving it with no escape route.

The rosette-spotted feline would have to do the unthinkable. It would have to fight its way out. It looked utterly hopeless for the smaller cat, and for a moment, the situation elicited a great deal of sympathy from the older children. The instinct to root for the underdog was always there. There was also a certain smugness masquerading as revenge in feeling the jaguar was getting its just desserts.

The pride for its part were in shock, slightly exhausted and not knowing quite how to subdue this small demon that they had chosen to pick a fight with. None of the pride wanted to go it alone with the jaguar. Two of the lionesses' tried again from opposite sides of the smaller cat. It was a half hearted attempt with neither lioness believing that it could do anything. Both lionesses backed away from the snarling feline demoness and made the tactical error of turning their backs on the jaguar.

In an unexpected move, within a flash, the jaguar threw itself onto one of the female lions ... clawing and biting before it leapt off the stunned cat. The entire pride leapt back ... somewhat startled. This little demoness had lots of fight in it. The two lionesses were so unnerved that they quickly withdrew from the scene. The other two big male lions backed off slowly then, turned and trotted off after the two females.

The jaguar headed into the opposite direction forgetting entirely about the three children up in the oak tree. The four lions stopped abruptly when they spotted the older children. All four giant lions were now staring directly at the children on the open grassland and then, the pride whipped their tails in the air and scampered off at a full run, away from the children.

Devin turned around to look behind them and yelled...

"OH SHIT!!! OH SHIT!!!"

Daniel and Beverly whipped around with the rest of the little band of children only to face eight more giant cats racing head long in the snow towards them. It was a veritable blizzard of snow as the big cats were almost upon them.

Devin instinctively yelled ... "Close ranks!!!"

The three spear holders were down on their knees ready to impale the big cats if they leapt upon them. The three children with their bows drawn back tight with at least one arrow on each bow began to relax the tightness' of their bow strings as the lions parted around them in pursuit of the other pride who had wandered into their territory. Territorial defence ... not hunger was the main drive behind the attack of the resident pride. All the children breathed a huge sigh of relief. Some were trembling. Some had once again peed themselves silly. No one seemed to notice. Everyone was glad to be alive ... still. As the resident pride disappeared chasing the intruders, the children made a run for the oak.

Within six minutes, they were all up in the lean-to excitedly talking about another life and death situation that they had wandered into and just barely survived. It was becoming quite clear to the children that they were surviving only because they were sticking it out together.

But another thought was now being discussed among them. The three younger children could no longer be left alone defenceless. Something had to be done about their situation. They wouldn't have the strength to use a bow, nor could they create new metal tip spear heads.

It was Gordon who had the ingenious idea of a brand new weapon ... one they could create with far greater ease. It was a weapon used for millennia and a dangerous one at that.

At the time the jaguar was at the base of their tree, flexing its muscles to roar up the side of the oak to grab the children, Gordon actually thought of dropping some burning firewood down on top of the cat. The three younger children had kept the morning fire going after breakfast. Now ... a plan was hatched among the older children.

It was conceived that they would shape a couple of eight foot pieces of wood and tie some smaller two foot pieces to one end of such a pole ... in a bundle. Slits would be made in the trunk of the oak or any other tree for that matter ... even cutting off a branch or tree limb. Sap in the form of resin would flow from the wound on the tree and be collected onto the end of the bundle. The entire bundle would be soaked in this resin and left out to dry for a week. Even the hemp that would be used to bind the bundle to the eight foot pole would be soaked in this sap. It was like glue and burned ferociously.

"Perhaps ..." Georgi thought ... "we should place these all around the base of the oak at night to keep predators away from us when we were most vulnerable".

For the rest of the afternoon Beverly, Benny and Georgi sat down to pluck the feathers of the three, forty pound birds. The gizzards, liver and heart were saved as delicacies while the insides of one of the birds was stuffed with different edible berries collected from around the forest.

The other two birds were kept partially frozen in the snow.

Dandelions were collected for tea.

The other older boys began the arduous task of making a dozen firebrands. They were going to be well protected this time. They were also going to feast like royalty, thanks to Beverly's knowledge of all things botanical.

By the end of the day, a stuffed bird was being rotated on a spit up in the lean-to, ten firebrands had been created, and by tomorrow, the resin would be collected as feul. In addition to all this, a third new hide was tied to the trunk of the oak for tomorrow's defleshing and tanning.

Tonight, for the first time, the children actually stuffed themselves. They were immensely satisfied. They had a mammoth rug underneath them and a mammoth hide over top of them for added warmth. The other hide tied to the oak was for mukluks or shoes, leggings and jackets.

Beverly was to teach everyone how to sew. Henry's diary also showed how to do it and it wasn't just mammoths that Henry worked on.

The puppies were well fed and snuggled together in their little lean-to below the children. For this night, it was a special occasion and against Devin, Beverly and Jacob's wishes. The puppies were brought into the upper lean-to to sleep once again with the children.

During the night, Mammoths quietly continued to migrate several hundred yards off on the other side of the waterway. The procession continued night and day. Sometimes the stressful calls of a young mammoth at night would bellow out as it was taken down by what sounded like the growls of a large pride of lions achieving dinner. The children themselves had earned the right to be part and parcel of this strange new world. They were truly on their own now and slowly but surely were empowering one another.

For children to do this without adult supervision was enlightening ...save the directions of Henry's diary which was by far their most important weapon to date.

. . .

Manfred instinctively turned the truck around and raced back towards town. As he neared the grain elevators in front, he slowed his vehicle and parked it off the main drag pulling up beside the towering structures. His heart was pounding. Could it be? Could the damn railcar that graced the Morley slough for over a century be sitting behind those grain elevators? He carefully opened his door and got out of his vehicle.

He felt the necessity to look around him to see if anybody else was watching. He closed his truck's door quietly and slowly began striding towards the buildings. He stopped as he reached them. He looked around one more time ... took a deep breath and disappeared between two of the elevators. It was like walking into a dark canyon he thought. It chilled him. It was as if the towering monoliths were going to slap shut on him.

He reappeared on the other side in the bright sunshine. He felt a surge of excitement. Still. He could be dead wrong about what he saw from half mile away. There was a row of boxcars in front of him. No caboose. That much he knew. It was at the back in the second row of railcars that he had seen it. He stepped between and out from two of the railcars. There it was ... at the end of the second row of some nine railcars. As he strode toward the caboose, his pace quickened. It was only three more railcars down but something was not quite right.

He made it to the caboose. It looked way too modern. He walked to the rear of the railcar to discover that what he thought he saw ... the lantern was in reality the flag hanging from the rear designating these railcars as part of a scheduled train. Manfred once again found himself shaking his head in how easily he was lead to jumping to conclusions. It paid off before but, maybe now, he had to start being more careful.

Manfred started to laugh ... "Here we go again" ... he thought.

Manfred never knew why he actually did it while standing there ... maybe intuition ... maybe an exploratory spirit but, he decided to move around to the other side of this semi-modern caboose. As he did so, he felt a cold shudder. He stepped across the rails at the back of the caboose to the other side ... and looked up.

There, half way down from the second row of railcars, sitting by itself on a third rail siding was an ancient looking caboose ... with a lantern hanging on the back ... a very ancient lantern. Manfred didn't know whether or not to approach the thing. He knew he had to. Once again his heart was racing. He walked cautiously down between the rails. The slow sixty metre walk sent chills up his spine. Manfred's heart was racing so fast that he found himself breathing rapidly. He had to relax but that was hard to do because he had no idea just what he was about to walk into ... and he had no survival gear with him.

He stopped within five feet of the ancient railcar. The lantern had no wick. He grabbed the rear hand rail and hoisted himself up. He was now standing at the front door of this railcar. He took one last look around, opened the door and stepped in. It was as he remembered it.

Manfred turned and backed out. His knees felt weak. He swung off the front platform and landed on the ground in front of the caboose. It felt reassuring. He had to think. He had to call Charlie.

Manfred raced away between the railcars on the other two sidings behind the towering grain elevators and was back in his truck.

Should he notify the Morden Society? No. First he had to communicate with Charlie Hadquil. Once back in Pilot Mound, he dropped back into Albert's house and phoned Charlie. Cynthia answered. Charlie was out finishing up on an 18-hole golf tournament.

"He should be back in about three hours"... Cynthia related.

Manfred thanked her and hung up. For the next three hours, Manfred resigned himself to going through some of Albert's notes.

. . .

The next morning the children awoke early and shoved more small pieces of kindling onto the main block of wood. The fire in their lean-to once more sputtered to life. Jacob and Beverly put on tea and made a little breakfast of berries mixed with pieces of last night's bird. The smell of tea and warm food awakened the other children.

Georgi and Benny carried the puppies back down to their smaller lean-to. The puppies were now ten weeks old. They were still too young to be trained but that was coming. It was too dangerous not to train them. Beverly had watched many films on training dogs. The training was left to her capable hands.

MAKING PLANS

Within a week, all the hide from the legs of that last mammoth had been cut up and sewed together to create one piece pull-overs for the three smaller children. They were tied at the waist. Two other older children had been similarly clothed in mammoth hide. The older children knew they had to bring down another two mammoths. They only needed the hide that would be exposed. The scavengers could take the rest.

It would give them enough to make even mukluks for their feet as well as crude mittens and virtually clothe them all. It also meant another dangerous foray out into the grasslands. It was something that they had to take very seriously.

Another mammoth hunt was necessary. The giants were still migrating. The giant predators were still bringing them down out across on the other side of the streambed. The window of opportunity was closing rapidly. They had to be ready for the next group and this time they had to be ready to drop not one but two giants. The thrill was there and it was always intoxicating and they were always lucky. This time, they could be injured or even killed. No one wanted to think about it. Everyone had to.

Devin brought up the unthinkable. With the migration window closing fast, they may have to be ready for a night hunt.

Beverly turned to Devin...

"Are...you...kidding Devin?!?...Out there, AT NIGHT!?!"

Everyone shifted their gaze from Beverly back to Devin. Some of the children were slack jawed at the suggestion. Others with contorted faces as to suggest Devin had just stepped out of La-la land. Devin wished he hadn't come up with such a concept. He was getting embarrassed as everybody was staring at him for not considering the potential dangers involved.

Georgi was the first to speak up ... "Devin could be right."

Benny looked at Georgi ... "What?!? Georgi!?! Those giant predators are all out there hunting at night. That's ... their time ... not ours."

Georgi countered ... "Precisely why we have to do it! They're hunting at night because that's when we hear their prey coming through this area ... and they're not going to be out there every single night. We saw the huge pile of bones and skeletons lying out there from our tree top. That's when most of them pass through this area. We should be out there ... no matter how dangerous."

"Right!" Beverly reiterated in a derisive way as she rolled her eyes and turned her head away as if dismissing the whole idea of night hunting.

Jacob spoke up quietly but with serious intent...

"Georgi might be right. We don't really know how many more chances we're going to get at this migration thing that the mammoths have going. Perhaps we ... SHOULD ... start planning?!? Any ideas? ...Anyone?"

He could see by the startled looks on everyone's face that they had not given this any thought. It was nothing short of suicide. In the darkness, the predators could be almost on top of them before any of them were even aware they were there. Then there's the possibility that they could shoot each other in that same darkness. They wouldn't know where everybody else was. And finally, what if one of the giants actually turned on them? It could turn to complete chaos out there. People would die.

Benny had an idea...

"All the uncertainties could be avoided if we could see in the dark ...Right?"

Jacob grabbed at Benny's thought "...The firebrands'!!"

Beverly turned to Jacob...

"...They'll see us coming a mile off ... Jake."

Devin lit up ... "We got twelve firebrands. We only need six out there. We leave the other six up in the lean-to just in case Gordon, Vera and Di-Di need a couple."

"We only need three out there"... Daniel called out...

"You can't use a bow while carrying a firebrand!!"

Everyone nodded in agreement.

"So" ... Daniel continued ... "we do it as couples. Spearman carries the firebrand. Bowman protects the spearman. Spearman tosses firebrand to bowman while going into attack mode. Once the spearman's job is done, he plants the firebrand next to the dead mammoth. Okay everyone??"

Silence greeted Daniel's words. Everyone thought carefully about the idea. Georgi started to giggle uncontrollably. Daniel was annoyed.

"I can see it all now" ... Georgi started ... "throwing the firebrands back and forth at each other ... everybody yelling, screaming running around ... I'm on fire !! Help!! I'm on fire!! Six guys running around like torches scaring away all the animals."

At that moment, everyone burst out laughing and repeating Georgi's words over and over.

Even Daniel ... who was not the least amused began chuckling and then, finally, joining the raucous laughter. When all finally became silent in the amber glow of their fire...

Daniel was still chuckling...

"Good one Georgi. So, aside from the dangers of turning ourselves into Georgi torches"...

Everyone once again started to giggle even though Daniel had not meant to stir up that ridiculous scenario. But it was funny ... very funny.

Beverly interjected. "We have to kill two of them before we start to skin the hide off any of them ...otherwise the carcasses will be too far apart for us to protect them."

Devin threw a thought out at them...

"Why not take down two at the same time? It may be slower but we could protect both kills if we brought them down together."

Benny chimed in ... "and exactly how do you propose we do that?"

Devin answered ... "one spearman on each mammoth with the third spearman running back and forth to help the other two. It would take longer but the animals would almost be side by side."

Daniel broke in ... "It's the safety part I'm worried about. If we don't take them down quickly, these giants might get enraged and literally turn on us. Then we're in trouble."

"Maybe we should only do one giant a night"... Beverly shot back.

"It would be a lot safer" ... Jacob declared to the group.

The decision was made...one mammoth, one night. No more. It was otherwise too risky.

. . .

Manfred went over Albert's books and noticed that Albert had circled some of the Stages in the geological time chart and made notes pertaining to the time he spent in each Stage.

But an inconsistency arose. Albert indicated he had spent close to twenty years on this adventure in the past. He would have been over fifty years old when he returned. He was only thirty ... the same age when he left ... but no one had noticed his disappearance.

Even more stunning was the fact that Albert himself would have noticed nothing had changed from his own perspective. This is why, Manfred thought, that Albert was unsure as to whether he had simply dreamed it all up. Then a truly frightening revelation hit Manfred.

If what Albert did was real, doesn't that mean that in all those years that have now passed, all the events leading up to now would simply be erased? Nobody would know.

The children would know but no one else would know. But what happened to the three railroad men that once accompanied the late great Charlie Stensis?

Manfred sat bolt upright when the phone rang, practically falling off his chair. It was Charlie. Manfred explained what he had found out on one of the side tracks behind the grain elevators in Larvyer. There were a few moments of silence before Charlie agreed to meet Manfred but, it would have to be the following morning at ten o'clock. They would meet at the Barclay's. Manfred leaned back and sighed. He was relieved.

Manfred's next thought was to look for his gear out on the slough and then to contact Eduard. In his excitement, in the early morning to get home, Manfred had driven right past the slough on the perimeter highway on his way to Pilot Mound. He forgot to take the dirt road off-pass on his way up out of the valley from Larvyer.

After leaving Albert's old house in Pilot Mound, Manfred jumped into his pick-up and headed out to the slough ... about a ten mile drive. He had forgotten to phone Eduard... again.

CHASING THE DEVIL

Manfred had arrived down at the slough. The area around where the ancient caboose once sat was taped off as an archaeological dig site. He parked his truck on the old municipal road across from the site. There was only a single tent off the road on the edge of the slough by the site. A security guard was on site using the tent.

Manfred clambered out of his truck and walked down off the road and across the edge of the slough to the tent. He stopped outside the tent door and called out. No answer. So he opened the tent flap and peered in, no one there. He backed out and looked around. He saw the security guard in the distance on the other side of the slough watching him.

The guard had decided to explore around the slough out of sheer boredom. He had a pair of binoculars and a two way radio with him to contact his base. Manfred ignored him and walked to the area where he had left his gear near the caboose.

The guard, now alarmed by Manfred's presence was cutting across the slough in a run. Manfred reached the exact spot where he had left all his gear. It was gone. To avoid a confrontation, Melvin immediately walked back to the tent and waited for the guard. He had a few questions of his own to ask.

Charlie kissed Cynthia goodbye and left the house. He would be there by ten o'clock in the morning as promised. Cynthia thought that this was such a silly goose chase on both their parts. Charlie understood this but Cynthia wasn't on that site when it happened.

Charlie had seen something happen out there that needed an explanation. It was beginning to have a grip on him that he couldn't loosen. He couldn't shake off the idea that a great and wonderful machine of extraordinary power once laid out under the cover of the Morley slough. If it was, then, no one on Earth could have built it. For the first time in his life, Charlie let the idea of an extraterrestrial origin brush by his mind. He quickly dismissed it. The explanation had to be simpler and more down to Earth. This was not the time to jump to fantastical scenarios. He needed more data otherwise this was going to bother him for a long, long time.

Besides, he rather enjoyed working on and solving problems. That's why he became the western chief mechanic for Air Canada. It was his calling and what Manfred presented to him was actually quite intoxicating.

. . .

The children organized themselves for an early sleep regimen. They had to be ready to leave at a moments notice. After dinner, the plans were drawn up and everyone knew their position in the field. Eight giant cave lions were nothing to take lightly but, this time, they would have fire. The light powdered snow on the grasslands would help to dampen down the possibility of the children setting everything ablaze accidentally.

The children were nervous. It was hard for them to sleep that night. As night fell, the distant trumpeting of the giants could be heard. Gordon, Di-Di and Vera were quite excited by the noise out in the grasslands. It meant...a hunt would soon commence. For the others, the sounds were met more with dread.

There was another problem to ponder and very carefully. Crossing the streambed filled with crocodiles. Daniel believed that the coming winter would be more like a cold fall, otherwise, how could the crocs possibly survive this inclement weather? The crocs were obviously as deep into a temperate zone as Nature would allow these "cold bloods."

According to Albert's mercury thermometer, the temperature almost never dropped below zero ... hence the light powdering of snow. During the day it would rise to 26-28 degrees C [85-90 degrees F]. It was a wild temperature fluctuation but, otherwise, it was quite warm, even hot sometimes. The only crossing point would be that dangerous point bar where a large brute of a croc called home. A night crossing might be safer when the giant reptiles were far more sluggish.

At night, as the trumpeting got louder with each approaching giant, the children at once recognized that something had changed. The calling out of one giant to another was different ... the pitch was higher. The children had never heard it before. Jacob, Beverly and Daniel were a little concerned. The darkness had now concealed a major change amongst the trumpeting giants. Unknown to the children, the cows were in oestrus while the enormous bulls were in rut or what was commonly known as musk.

These animals were no longer the gentle giants, easy to take down creatures they were before. These animals now were extremely dangerous and would give chase to anything that moved anywhere in their environment.

. . .

Charlie arrived on top of the prairie escarpment in Larvyer a few minutes before ten. The drive down the winding highway into the Pembina Valley where the tiny hamlet of Larvyer was located was quite a scenic drive with the escarpment falling away from the side of the road into a very deep ravine. Charlie arrived at the bottom in Larvyer and slowly drove up to the old Barclay hotel and bar, scanning the front of this hotel for Manfred's parked pick-up truck. It was there. Charlie exited from his vehicle and strode into the door of the hotel. The bell chime went off as he pushed the door open. He scanned the restaurant for Manfred. There were perhaps only a dozen tourists there all together but ... no Manfred. Charlie got himself seated at a table not far from the door and waited. A pretty middle aged waitress walked up and gave him a menu and a cup of coffee with cream, sugar on a different plate.

Charlie ordered eggs, bacon, toast and a little jam on the side. Charlie was sure that was Manfred's truck sitting outside the hotel. At that moment, Manfred walked in from the washroom. He greeted Charlie and mentioned that he had just arrived himself and was eager to show Charles the ancient railcar behind the elevators. Charlie motioned him to sit down and order. Manfred ordered the same as Charlie plus orange juice. Manfred explained what he had found and Charlie related to Manfred what he thought.

"If any of this is true" ... Charlie related to Manfred... "then the core machine 10,000 feet in circumference acted as a power source. The caboose ..." as Charlie tried to explain to Manfred ... "acted as a device ... some kind of device that required a recharge of sorts ... like a battery ... to continue to operate and do god only knows what. Well, that's my best guess."

Then Charlie added ... "This thing ... this caboose, could be fully charged ... and if it was ... anything could happen".

Manfred was temporarily stunned. Charlie had come full circle to entertain that these events were, quite possibly, from outside of this world. Charles even wondered aloud if they were dealing with a wormhole. When Manfred asked what that was, Charlie waved his hand in a dismissive way...

"...Just thinking out loud."

. . .

At about nine, according to Albert's time piece left in one of the backpacks with the rest of his gear, the kids steeled themselves for the task at hand. They clambered down their oak tree while petting the pups as they slipped past them.

The pups for their part started to whimper at the prospect of being left behind. Vera and Di-Di took the puppies up to the main lean-to. There were no steps between the lean-tos so that the pups couldn't get down by themselves. It was a way of locking them into the oak while the older kids were gone hunting and gathering.

The older children made their way from the base of the oak out into the grasslands. Across on the other side of the stream, the older kids could make out the dark silhouettes of the giants wandering past nearly two hundred yards out. It was going to be a long walk.

. . .

As they ate breakfast and drank their coffee, Manfred thought he could hear a steam locomotive rumble into Larvyer. A few minutes later he could hear the crash of railcars being moved around. Manfred paid the bill and hurriedly told Charlie to move faster ... something was happening in the rail yard behind the grain elevators. Charlie could see Manfred was beginning to panic and so hurried along but instructed Manfred to go across Main Street to the elevators to see what was happening. He would meet Manfred shortly after a jaunt to the bathroom. Manfred left a tip on the table and bolted out the door to his pick-up. He roared out of the tiny parking lot, drove a block down Main Street and over to the grain elevators. He had barely stopped and shut off the truck engine when he flew out the door of his vehicle. He was running between the grain elevators and burst out into the sun light. He could hear the railcars crashing and interlocking, then ... the locomotive putting on a burst of power. He looked both ways down the first bank of railcars to make certain there wasn't a locomotive on either end. He leapt between two of the railcars. The second rack of railcars had been taken out by the diesel already. His heart skipped a beat when he saw the ancient caboose on the rear of the train. He panicked and ran after it waving frantically. The train had picked up too much speed. Manfred stopped dead.

He whipped around and ran back to his pick-up. He had no chance of stopping the train. He drove directly to the station agent assigned to Larvyer. It was only a block down from the grain elevators. Manfred burst through the doors of the railroad station. There were about half a dozen people vying for the attention of the station agent.

Manfred excused himself and interrupted the ongoing conversation. He had to know where that last train was going and why it had picked up that caboose.

At that moment the station agent turned to Manfred in astonishment...

"You're Manfred Morley!! Aren't you?!?"

Ever polite, Manfred clarified that he did not have time to discuss anything except this incident with that last train. Manfred asked if he could see the manifest for the pickup of those railcars. The station agent told Manfred under no circumstance could he discuss the details of the manifest ... only the destination. That destination was the even smaller hamlet of Mather.

It was then that the station agent remarked...

"What caboose are you referring to Mr. Morley? There is no caboose here to pick up."

Manfred stopped short ... "But you're Engineer just picked one up!!"

"We've never seen a caboose here Mr. Morley" ... the station agent stammered...

"What are you talking about?"

Flabbergasted, Manfred turned and pointed to the spot where the caboose had just stood for the last day or so. The station agent took a step back in shock.

It was then that one of the men in the station spoke up.

"Yah ... I remember that railcar ... a caboose ... a really old one ... by itself on the outside rail."

The man turned to an astonished station agent who was now rifling through the manifest...

"I saw it yesterday."

The station agent slowly shook his head ... "Nothing on this manifest says anything about a caboose."

The door slammed open. Manfred was gone. He bumped into Charlie and yelled for him to get in his car. The caboose was on the back of a train heading to Mather. He and Charlie needed to intercept it.

Charlie threw his hands in the air while thinking to himself...

"This is ridiculous!"

But Charles resigned himself...

"Well ... I'm here now ... let the chase begin"... as he turned and raced to his car to follow Manfred.

He was going to give Manfred an earful if either one of them got a ticket for speeding as the two vehicles rocketed up to the top of the escarpment overlooking Larvyer.

. . .

Daniel, Devin and Beverly reached the stream bank nearest the mudflat or point bar. It was dark. They had just passed the body of the giant cat that had received that first arrow in the shoulder blade. The body had been cleaned up by vultures. Only a skeleton remained.

It reminded Daniel of the pictures in his fossil books back home in another place and another time, something he might have seen mounted in a museum. The children however had the privilege of seeing and actually interacting with the real thing.

"That was something"... he thought.

As the children gathered across from the sand bar, they scoured the waters for any crocs. It was almost impossible to see in the darkness. It was pretty narrow on both sides of the sand bar. The three archers readied their bows.

The other three simply ran into the knee deep water and up onto the sand bar. Each of the three archers followed. There was a lot of splashing which alarmed Beverly...too much splashing. Still, no sign of any crocs. The crossing to the other side of the stream bed went without incident.

With three torches in hand, they made their way into the deep grasslands toward the silhouetted giants. As the children closed the gap between themselves and the giants, it was becoming clear to the little band of child hunters that there was something different about the giant mammoths. The tusks of these giants were different. They weren't so curved but rather straighter than the giants they had previously seen. They weren't as tall either. Their shoulders weren't higher than their rear ends. In fact, as the child hunters noticed, their shoulders were no higher than their rear ends. It gave them pause. The child hunters were within thirty yards of the column of elephantine giants.

The young hunters froze where they stood. These weren't mammoths. On closer inspection, Georgi and Daniel recognized these new giants as Mastodons. The whole troupe buzzed with the excitement that they had just discovered another kind of prehistoric giant. One giant in the migratory herd stopped. The child hunters had temporarily forgotten where they were.

Their excited chatter didn't sit well with this one large mastodon, a bull, and he was having nothing of this. The giant turned its head and great tusks towards the children. Now five giant bull mastodons had stopped. Three of the five giants turned their great heads towards the little troupe of hunters.

Two of the giant bulls flung their huge trunks skyward, raised their lethal tusks into the air and trumpeted again. The child hunters had not yet caught on as to what was happening. They were watching these great beasts as if they were flipping through a National Geographic magazine ... totally disconnected from the scene.

The first bull made the connection for them.

It charged.

. . .

Manfred and Charlie drove the ten miles to Pilot Mound, then passed Crystal City, turned off the main highway before the town of Boissevain and headed towards the little hamlet of Mather. Manfred and Charlie had arrived before the train that was towing their strange caboose. They pulled off the road by the railroad-track-crossing inside the small town. It was a town of fifty to sixty people at most, quiet, ghostlike.

Eduard and Anastasia Morley once operated and lived in the railroad station beside the tracks, across from the grain elevators years ago, with their two children ... Samuel and Suzanne. There was talk that the station and elevators were to be torn down and the railroad torn away from the town soon. Manfred sighed. All across this great land, nothing was being saved of their cultural history. It was all being torn down ... one town after the other. They looked around them.

All these towns, thought Manfred, they were all destined to become ghost towns ... like his farm. Within fifty years, there would be nothing left to even mark that there ever was a town here. He sighed again ... deeply.

They had decided to park discreetly away from the train station and waited. They didn't have to wait long. The train was coming. It was a freight train as expected. Manfred and Charles were watching for the number on the locomotive to be sure they had the right train. As the locomotive slowed its approach into the town to drop off seven boxcars on a siding track next to the grain elevators, Manfred and Charlie eagerly anticipated seeing the caboose at the end of the sixty railcar train. Manfred still couldn't understand why the locomotive engineer picked up the unscheduled caboose in the first place. It made him uneasy. The engineer, thought Manfred, was going directly against the rules of the railroading community. The engineer had no manifest whatsoever to couple that caboose onto the end of that train. As the train slowly passed the crossing, Charlie noticed that there was no caboose attached to this train. Manfred was astonished. When the train stopped, both men could clearly see that no caboose was attached. Charlie slowly turned and looked at Manfred ... waiting for an explanation.

Manfred interjected ... "That customer picking up a package at the Larvyer station distinctly told me that locomotive 2031 picked up that caboose. I'm going to talk to this Engineer before he leaves.

Manfred began running down the long line of freight cars towards the lead engine.

Charlie, for his part, rushed over to the two brakemen to plead with them to delay signalling the engineer until Manfred had had the time to talk with him. Manfred ... exhausted, had reached the lead locomotive. He waved his hands and started to yell to get the engineer's attention.

The locomotive engineer leaned out the window as Manfred yelled out his introduction to him and threw his question up to the engineer. Leaning out the window, the engineer told Manfred that he had an odd message from dispatch in Larvyer about that caboose. The Engineer explained to Manfred that everyone had seen that strange looking caboose but, they never stopped to pick it up.

Manfred thanked the Engineer. Charlie, for his part, asked one of the brakemen if they had seen that odd looking caboose in Larvyer. The brakeman said they had seen it but thought nothing of it ... thought it was being refurnished as a tourist attraction for the town.

By the time Manfred walked back, the train had left the little hamlet of Mather.

Manfred stopped in front of Charlie and sighed deeply. Manfred bowed his head, placed his hands on his hips and exclaimed, in a half defeated voice...

"Now what are we going to do??"

Charlie looked into Manfred's face...

"I was thinking. This thing, the caboose, is fully charged. It could be self-mobilized. Perhaps it coupled itself to the train as the locomotive left Larvyer and then later decoupled in a passing town to hide out among the stacks of railcars ... who knows??"

Charlie thought to himself...

"This is the best he could come up with??"

There was a central bank in Mather where Manfred made a call to the Larvyer station agent who was posted there. He reintroduced himself to the station agent and related how he and Charlie followed that train out to Mather and found, to their disappointment, that no caboose was attached.

The Larvyer station agent once again was left scratching his head over this odd occurrence of an unknown caboose that left his rail yard. Manfred received a list of small towns that the train passed through. He and Charlie decided to drive to every one of those towns which numbered close to seven small hamlets that train locomotive 2031 intersected.

"They were chasing the devil's train"... thought Charlie.

It was getting kind of spooky. More and more, he and Manfred were being drawn into this thing. Charles found he was actually hooked on the excitement. It was a good mystery even if it turned out to be benign. Even the Morden Society was out searching for it when the CPR failed to find it in Larvyer for transport to Morden.

There were warnings in the news of severe weather conditions involving some unexpected, very high winds. By noon hour, driving the old highway between the small hamlets of Holland and Treherne, parallel to the railroad tracks, Manfred and Charlie both noticed an unusual sight adjacent to the highway. On the tracks, exactly halfway between those two towns, an orange-red railcar was sitting serenely by itself on a sidetrack. It sent chills up Charlie's spine. No one on these CPR lines had any idea of the whereabouts of this strange looking caboose from a bygone era yet, here it sat, alone, beckoning, even daring anyone to approach it.

Manfred slowed his pickup and gently cruised over to the side of the highway, onto the gravelled shoulder, parallel to the caboose.

Charlie pulled his vehicle up behind Manfred's pickup. They both cut their engines.

For nearly half a minute neither man moved, being quite unsure of what to do exactly. How should they explore this? Manfred climbed out of his pickup. Charlie followed. They looked across at one another. Now what? Charlie walked up to Manfred.

"Well. We came this far. I see an invitation to explore this thing, you?"

Manfred took a deep breath...

"...Right! Let's do this."

He looked around. They were totally alone out here. No witnesses. Manfred turned back to the railcar and pondered...

"It just seems to be sitting there ... waiting for us ... like an open bear trap."

He shuddered.

Both men left their car doors unlocked since they were miles away from any nearby town. Neither one had anything of value in their vehicles. Manfred, in his hurry, had even left the door to his pickup open. Charlie noticed this and reminded him. Manfred waved it off. Both men started to gingerly climb down the embankment of tall grass towards the bottom of the seemingly dry gulch.

There was just a telltale sign of the wind picking up. It was just a slight breeze, a very warm breeze. It did nothing to cool the hot summer sun bearing down on them. Both men struggled up through the long dry grass to the railroad trestle and into the shadow of the railcar. It loomed over them like some ancient sentinel.

Manfred could feel a certain coolness to the breeze coming from under the dark carriage of the railcar.

Charlie's heart was throbbing a little harder due to the climb up to the railcar and his excitement over the most unusual circumstances surrounding this orange-red object of so much speculation.

Manfred's heart was beating too, even pounding, far harder than it should, given that the climb up to the trestle for a man in his shape was nothing at all. It was adrenaline ... the pure adrenaline, produced in the human body from ... fear.

. . .

The conversation among the excited children came to an abrupt halt. The bull mastodon reminded Georgi of a locomotive on a railroad ploughing through deep snow. You don't want to be standing anywhere in front of it. The children began backing up.

Then, they were in a full run staying tightly together in the dark. The children were about to part to scatter every which way when the colossus abruptly stopped its charge. It could have easily run them down with no effort on its part but, it was having difficulty seeing them in the dark. It also had a harem of females to protect against other younger bulls. This terrifying charge showed the children just how dangerous it had now become to hunt these giants.

"These are far more dangerous animals. They won't let us anywhere near them. I think we should quit"... Beverly complained

"...this is just way too crazy."

Jacob and Daniel looked around at their already startled troupe. Just then, a large bull let out a trumpet call and charged the big bull that had sent their little crew running. The two giants hit head on and interlocked their great tusks. They were in a shoving match. One giant took a couple of steps back and a deadly fencing match with tusks was underway.

The clacking of tusk against tusk was loud. The grunting and wheezing of the giants could be heard above the trumpeting of other giants.

"What's going on here" ... Daniel asked in bewilderment.

Beverly began to giggle ... "You don't know?"

Georgi turned to Beverly ... "What's so funny?"

Beverly waved off Georgi's question with an embarrassed smile.

Devin then interjected ... "The two big ones fighting are big bulls. The others are cows ... females. It's must be their mating season. They're trying to find out who the strongest bull is, so that the cows will only mate with him. That way, their babies are going to be the strongest in their land. Each generation keeps getting bigger and stronger or just healthier.

That's how my dad explained it to me. That's when they'll pick a fight with anything that moves, just to impress the lady cows how fast and strong they are in order to protect the herd."

"So ... just how long does this last Devin?" Daniel asked timidly.

"It can last for weeks ... up to a month ... but usually not longer than that" ... Devin intimated.

At that moment, a large bull mastodon toppled over. It had been gored. The other big bull continued to charge it repeatedly goring it again and again. The mastodon on the ground wheezed, lifted up his head and tusks silently then slammed its head back onto the ground. No sound. No movement. It was badly injured. The other young bulls backed away. The old bull trumpeted loudly as it stood over the younger dying bull. It was over.

The herd wasn't moving on.

"Now's our chance!!"

Benny whispered loudly looking around at the others.

Daniel looked at Jacob.

Jacob looked up sharply...

"Let's do this!!"

Without waiting, he took the lead grabbing the torch from Benny. It was the only way to get everybody going once again before they could talk themselves out of it. The little troupe of child hunters resigned themselves to continuing the hunt. They were all relieved by the fact that they didn't have to bring down their own mastodon. Still, they had to be very careful. Big angry giants, single or even packs of predators and the darkness all made for a most dangerous evening. They carefully ran then, walked to the downed carcass of the mastodon, approaching it slowly so as to not alarm the big bulls around them who were looking to pick a fight with anything that moved out there in the grasslands. They approached the rear of the mastodon lying on its side and began poking it with their spears ... thrusting deeply. There was no movement or heavy breathing. It appeared to have expired. The troop looked at each other then poured themselves up and onto the mastodon while others stood with the torches and scanned their surroundings in the pitch blackness that had descended upon them.

Everyone was extremely nervous.

The hide was finally removed and a large chunk of meat had been removed from the thigh to eat for dinner if and when the little troop got back to the relative safety of their oak ... if they could find it in the dark. That too was worrisome. It was imperceptible at first, but Beverly thought she had heard a snarl in the distance. She stood up as the rest of the crew was rolling up the hide.

Then there were several snarls from all around them.

None of the children could hear it. Beverly intensely yelled in a loud whisper...

"SHHHHHHHHHHH!!!"

Everyone froze. No one breathed. Then a cacophony of extremely loud snarls from all around them in the darkness ensued. It sounded like a very large number of predators had quietly, with great stealth and deliberation, completely surrounded them. The darkness all around them lit up with pairs of glowing yellow eyes ... first five or six pairs ... now two dozen or more. They were everywhere. The child hunters had let their guard down during the worst moment possible.

They were being surrounded by a circle of death's very own demons of the Holocene world. The child hunters, terrified, grouped together with the torch bearers on the outside of their tiny formation and gradually backed off from the mastodon carcass. They recognized immediately by the deafening dog-like snarls that they had been successfully surrounded by a very large pack of Dire wolves. There was no chance of fighting that many off. Unarmed ... just one of these brutes was fully capable of killing all six children together.

Their fiery torches were the only weapon that gave them any chance and it was strictly a psychological weapon to be used against these primitive brutes. The children swished the torches back and forth around them. The children with the bows stood ready. The children with the spears flashed their spear points back and forth in the torch light. There was, among the child hunters, the thought that this was not going to turn out very well for any of them.

If they died here, Gordon, Vera and Di-Di would be left sadly on their own.

If the Dires attacked them ... it would be over in less than thirty seconds and at that moment ... the Dires did just that. There was an imperceptible signal among these brutes. They launched their massive attack and the circle of nearly thirty Dire wolves surrounding the child hunters closed instantly with every Dire focused on overwhelming their prey.

END GAME

The wind had picked up some. Manfred remembered on the truck radio that very severe winds could be expected for southern Manitoba. He had heard that hundred mile-per-hour winds could be expected in the area that they were within. He had only experienced that twice in his life. It would be dangerous to be outside, if that were the case. Manfred and Charlie stood up on the trestle directly beside the caboose and turned to look at each other.

Manfred decided to explore around inside. Charlie, for his part, decided to photograph the undercarriage. There was a strange looking devise that made up a fair amount of the undercarriage that he had no idea of what it actually represented. Manfred, armed with his own camera, decided to photo shoot the interior of the railcar.

As he stepped inside, he was overwhelmed by a rush of nostalgia. Manfred let his hand glide over the table and benches as a flood of memories from different times and different events cascaded through his mind like a waterfall. In the meantime, Charlie was inching his way around underneath the carriage photographing the strange anomaly he had discovered but, the dust was getting in his eyes and making it hard to see. He decided enough was enough.

The winds were becoming ferocious now as they blew at some forty five miles per hour.

It was too much. He would join Manfred in the caboose and wait out the storm. It shouldn't last too long, he thought. Charlie staggered up into the railcar to be with Manfred.

"Getting pretty wild out there now" ... Manfred exclaimed.

Charlie simply grunted as he peered out the rear window. The caboose was starting to violently rock on its shockers.

The wind had picked up. It was now blowing at seventy two miles per hour. Dirt and dust were blowing everywhere. It was almost impossible to see outside. Unknown to Manfred, the open door of his pickup had just snapped from its top hinge. The bottom door hinge was all that was holding it onto the truck's frame.

The now howling wind could be heard as it whipped the electrical utility wires back and forth on the poles lining the side of the railroad trestle. The sound the wires made was like a strange note, almost a siren sound that took Manfred's inner most thoughts back to the farm as a kid.

The wind had picked up and further increased its power yet again to eighty eight miles per hour. Both men were startled by the loud sound of cracking timber and the high pitched whoosh of wires severed from their harnesses on the utility poles.

The door to Manfred's truck had been severed clean off his pickup and was now sliding down the highway towards the hamlet of Treherne. A final crack of timber felled several utility poles down onto the railroad trestle sending up a shower of sparks, lighting up the darkened area with a blue glow. Great arcs of crackling electrical current could be seen by both men through the rear windows of the caboose. The electrical lines had fallen onto the rails ... charging them.

Manfred looked on in horror.

Without explaining, he grabbed Charlie...

"WE GOTTA GET OUT OF HERE ... NOW!!!"

Manfred flung the rear door of the railcar open and pulled Charlie outside.

Charlie yelled back to Manfred

"WATCH OUT FOR THE DOWNED WIRES!!!"

Manfred and Charlie were trying to fight their way against the powerful wind. They were barely able to move. The wind finally loosened its grip on the railcar, tumbling them both into the tall grass next to the train trestle.

Charlie's car had inadvertently slid in hops straight into the rear of Manfred's pickup with a resounding crash. The ninety three mile per hour wind kept both men on the ground shielding their faces.

Charlie thought to himself how utterly stupid it was to be out in the open. Manfred was terrified that they weren't far enough away from the railcar. It was at that moment the wind had died down almost instantly. Relieved, both men clambered to their feet and dusted themselves off.

"Do you mind telling me why you pulled both of us out of that railcar Manfred?"

Charlie could see, from the expression of terror on Manfred's face that, something else was happening. Charlie turned to glance at what Manfred was fixated upon.

The storm had not subsided. It was still wrecking havoc all around them. There was a huge dome of quiet extending some three thousand feet around the caboose. They were at the edge of the outer circle by the railcar. Both men noticed the circulating counter clockwise dust at the edge of the dome that they now found themselves within. There was an immediate chill that had descended upon them.

"...Manfred! Look!"

Manfred looked up at the sight that Charlie himself was fixated upon. Above them, an immense, brightly lit, multihued aurora of dazzling light arced above them. Then it was out. Both men turned to glance at each other.

The calm dissipated immediately as the ferocious winds raced in once more, slamming into the side of the railcar. The two men only a moment before had turned away to shield themselves from that onslaught as electrical static discharges covered their bodies. An extremely bright light that emanated from within the lantern on the rear of the caboose instantly seared its way out through the windows as if a small replica of the sun had appeared inside the railcar and then ... winked out.

. . .

The Dire wolves rushed in and passed the children. The children could almost touch them as the Dires passed the little band of intrepid explorers and then piled themselves upon the dead mastodon. It sent a chill up the spines of the children, as they heard but, could not see the sound of meat being ripped from the bones of the mastodon, among the loud cacophony of Dires, snarling and attacking one another over bits and chunks of meat. The children backed off quickly. The sounds were sure to bring other predators.

Now they had to start finding their way back in the pitch black darkness. Their saving grace was that they could still see the fire pit high in the oak. Devin was glad they never built an entirely enclosed lean-to. By midnight, the little rag-tag band of explorers was up and in their lean-to, exhausted but otherwise not the worst for wear. Some of them would be entertaining nightmarish dreams tonight.

In another world, three dogs that grew up isolated and antagonistic towards each other were now growing up as puppies, together, in the same pack, led by similar primates who themselves were little more than human pups. It was, for all practical purposes, a puppy pack of canines and primates striving to learn and survive in a hostile world of packs of adult killers.

It was three months now, and the puppies were still very young dogs at the still tender age of eighteen weeks. Both Mickey and Skipper hunted together as a pack, occasionally running down the odd rabbit or squirrel virtually on command.

They were being trained under the stewardship of Beverly. Towzer's personality was markedly different. He wasn't so snappy. He was a live and let live kind of dog ... much gentler than the other two ... and without much of a honed killer instinct. He was mostly play.

Beverly didn't mind. She trained him to carry things like bundles to and from fixed points. The three smaller kids were fascinated by their dogs' growing training under Beverly.

It was morning. It had been three months since their arrival in what could only be described as the very early Holocene ... a period in Earth's history stretching back some ten thousand years. The day was coming fast. It was only a few hours away at most. During last night, the child explorers had a rather intense discussion among themselves.

Do they go back to their original point of their arrival in this strange world, deep in the grasslands of the Cave Lion pride? Do they stay where they are ... snug and comfortable ... giving up any chance of ever returning to their own world?

That morning found all nine child explorers and their three canine pups standing at the base of their oak tree. It was hard to give up their new and well established home. They had fought so hard to build and maintain it. Daniel and Jacob and the rest of their ragtag group were anticipating their return to Morley Lake and their trek up to the farmhouse from the marshland to a home cooked meal and their family. Everyone was excited.

For one last final time, they lit their torches and one after the other, followed Jacob and Beverly into the grasslands, away from the safety of the oak. This time ... there was no turning back. They would be five thousand feet ... nearly an entire mile, out into the most dangerous area and circumstance that they could inject themselves into. Out there ... there was no where to go if they were ever attacked. They would have to sleep on the ground, even endure rain and hail if it came to that. Their torches would ignite the small bundle of wood to give them at best two nights.

Within an hour, the fledgling explorers had made it to their destination. They quickly set up camp. A tarpaulin given them by Uncle Albert, shielded the fire and crew. Most of the day passed uneventfully, relieved about this fact as they were. Night would soon fall.

They planted some ten unlit torches around their makeshift tepee created from the tarpaulin. It was ingenious of Uncle Albert to rig it up that way. Benny was glad he had grabbed the tarpaulin as a last thought before stepping off the caboose platform and into the grasslands. In late afternoon, they slowly devoured a luncheon of meat with a little fruit and then waited.

They could hear the distant roar of the giant male cats. The giant felines were getting aroused again....still no sign of any animals. Georgi was hoping it would stay that way. The children began yawning. Some simply lay back and began a restless sleep.

Mickey saw a rabbit in the tall grass around the campsite and instinctively took off to run it down. The pup was all baby fat, and by himself, Mickey had no chance of catching the creature. Beverly called for Mickey to return but to no avail. Mickey was still a pup and had a little bit of disciplining ahead of him. Georgi ran after him. He and Mickey were now about two hundred feet out. He was trying to be as quiet as he could but once in a while yelled out Mickey's name.

All of a sudden while everyone was watching, Georgi went down and disappeared in the long grass. Everyone gasped, expecting the worst. A moment later, he stood up holding Mickey over his head. As Georgi walked toward the group with Mickey in his arms, he was immediately startled by the fact that the children were pointing in his direction and screaming for him to run. Georgi froze and then whirled around.

Some fifteen heads had risen up out of the grassland about a hundred yards behind him. He was electrified.

They were Cro-Magnons.

Much more ominously, their ticket home was now being punched. A thin column of dust in the middle of the grasslands was rising quickly. It was a monster swirling whirl wind of huge proportions.

Georgi knew immediately what that meant. He dropped Mickey and yelled at the pup to run with him. The two were still a hundred yards from the edge of the colossal whirl wind with the Cro-Magnons now in close pursuit and closing the distance rapidly between them and Georgi. The first Cro-Magnon spear thrown from an atl plunged into the ground nearly fifty feet in front of Georgi. He was well within the range of their weapons. He began to zigzag to avoid being hit. This cost him time. The size of the whirl wind caused the warriors to slow. A brilliant aurora of multi-hued lights danced above them. They stopped. Georgi was still forty feet outside the dome of dust. It was now or never. He made a straight dash for the swirling monster.

The children were frantic. Already ... sparks of static electricity were dancing off the children and their equipment. He was at the outer rim of the cascading behemoth as seven of the Cro-Magnons loosed a final volley. Five of the spears entered the outer rim of the colossus with the Cro-Magnons only seventy yards away. Two spears found their target. Georgi's face contorted as he went down hard ... barely a hundred yards from his family. Every face wore a shocked mask as the aurora above them blinked out. A stabbing white light issued from a central point about where the caboose might have been. In that instant, Vera had turned away and momentarily glimpsed at what she thought were black shadowed silhouettes of two men also seemingly shielding themselves from the glaring light.

The monster dust devil fell instantly. The blinding light blinked out. The image all around them of the once familiar grasslands vanished.

NEW BEGINNINGS

The Provincial cruiser slowed and pulled up to a door of a pickup lying by itself on the highway a few miles outside of Treherne. Corporal Fred stepped out.

"Be with you in a minute Christine".

Fred walked over, grabbed the door and dragged it off the highway out of harm's way. Fred slipped back into the cruiser.

"Looks like it might belong to one of those two vehicles" Christine retorted.

"Looks like one piled into the other. Better radio it in. We're going to check it out" Fred stated.

As the cruiser made a wide U-turn in the middle of the highway and pulled up behind the second vehicle, Constable Christina automatically switched on the red and blues. Christine got out and took the licence plate numbers off the two vehicles. Fred was busy making out a couple of abandoned vehicle reports when Christina came back to Fred's open window. He immediately radioed in to have the plates checked.

While Central was doing that, he climbed out to join Constable Christina for a closer look at the two vehicles.

Fred turned to Christina after scanning the highway in both directions...

"Where'd the two drivers go?"

"Probably lit out to Treherne to make a couple phone calls" Christina responded.

Central Dispatch radioed back. Fred walked quickly back to their cruiser and dipped his head into his vehicle. Christina looked around the two vehicles, and then glanced up and down the highway. She was puzzled. Maybe they went to a farmhouse to call someone.

She checked their fuel.

They were still good to go. The damage was minor in that both vehicles were still drivable. Why would they walk?

"Hey, Christine!"

Corporal Fred approached her quickly.

"Guess what? The pickup belongs to one Manfred Morley while the other vehicle is Charlie Hadquil's. Christine ... those were the two guys who were at that dig with the Morden Museum Society. You know that strange railcar?"

Christine glanced one more time down the long stretch of highway

"...What were they doing way out here??"

As she turned back to Corporal Fred, she noticed a rather intense look on the corporal's face.

"Christine ..." he said, nodding at something behind her.

Christine slowly turned to face a railcar sitting idly by itself on the train trestle.

"It's a caboose..." she said softly.

"Not just any caboose, but a really ancient one" Fred stammered.

The two officers slowly turned to each other. Christine was the first to speak...

"You don't think..."

. . .

When only tendrils of the giant dust devil remained, did the child explorers slowly lift their heads and peer outwards through the dust, all the while straining to catch a glimpse of their marshland, their farms, the dusty roads and telephone poles. There were none to be seen. They were still in the grasslands ... but it was altered somewhat ... different. The topography of the landform had changed.

They began to quickly walk and then run towards the spot that they had last seen Georgi drop into the grasses. There was not a sign, even, of the dog, Mickey. Suddenly ... there was a loud crash that startled them all. Two giant armoured glyptodonts with massive spiked tails were duking it out barely a hundred and fifty feet to their left. It was not their immediate concern.

It was Georgi ... Georgi and Mickey were gone ... they didn't make it through. It was heartbreaking for everyone. Three of the children began to cry. The others were fighting the emotion off. They had to. They were once again vulnerable, in the middle of nowhere. With Georgi and Mickey gone, it wouldn't be the same anymore. For Daniel, it was a lesson for everyone at just how dangerous, how precarious their existence had become.

They turned slowly to face the giant glyptodonts and it was beginning to sink in, that none of them had really made it back ... for they were all truly lost, plunging downward through the catacombs of time ... facing a new world more ancient than the one they had just left behind.

They began to realise that their journey was just beginning.

****

If you'd like to learn more about 'Cesta Do Praveku' and the works of Karel Zeman, please contact:

Karel Zeman Museum
Saský dvůr – Saská 3, 118 00 Prague 1
Malá Strana
info@muzeumkarlazemana.cz
phone +420 724 341 091

Made in the USA
Columbia, SC
12 May 2017